# D: WHITBY'S DARKEST SECRET

*a novel by*

## CHRIS TURNBULL

This is a work of fiction. Names, characters, businesses, places, events and incidents are either the products of the author's imagination, or if real are used in a fictitious manner. Any resemblance to actual persons, living or dead, or actual events is purely coincidental.

ISBN: 9781516823802

First published 2015 by Follow This Publishing, Yorkshire (UK)
Text © 2015 Chris Turnbull
Cover Design © 2015 Incredibook Design

The right of Chris Turnbull to be identified as author of this work has been asserted by him in accordance with the Copyright, Design and Patents Act 1988.

*For Dawn & Pete*

## ALSO BY CHRIS TURNBULL

*The Vintage Coat*
*Carousel*

*D: Darkest Beginnings*
*D: Revenge Hits London*

*The Planting of the Penny Hedge*

*It's Beginning To Look A Lot Like Christmas*
*A Home For Emy*
*Emy Gets A Sister*

# Caedmon's Hymn

## Old English

Nu sculon herigean heofonrices Weard,
Meotodes meahte ond his modgeþanc,
weorc Wuldorfæder; swa he wundra gehwæs
ece Drihten, or onstealde.
He ærest sceop eorðan bearnum
heofon to hrofe, halig Scyppend:
þa middangeard moncynnes Weard,
ece Drihten, æfter teode
firum foldan, Frea ælmihtig.

## Modern Translation

Praise now to the keeper of the kingdom of
heaven,
the power of the Creator, the profound mind
of the glorious Father, who fashioned the
beginning
of every wonder, the eternal Lord.
For the children of men he made first
heaven as a roof, the holy Creator.
Then the Lord of mankind, the everlasting
Shepherd,
ordained in the midst as a dwelling place,
Almighty Lord, the earth for men.

# PROLOGUE

An enormous ear-piecing scream broke the deathly silence of the night. Footsteps echoed along the narrow street, loud and fast paced as they raced along the street. It was a woman running along the cobbled road crying for help, her face wet from tears that ran down her face, and dark streaks from the mascara that once framed her eyes. She knew perfectly well that people could hear her calls for help, but with the events of recent weeks, nobody dared to leave their houses. Midnight was fast approaching. The woman stopped running for a split second to re-catch her breath. It was another cold night, and her breath could be seen in the darkness before her face; the only light given from the full moon watching her in the clear sky above.

'Help me, please… anybody…!'

The young woman stopped in the doorway of one of the inns and began banging on the large old oak door; but nobody answered. Finally as the woman was beginning to admit defeat a gentleman emerged from the shadows and grabbed her by the arm.

'What is the matter my dear?' the tall man asked, his voice low and stern but the woman could see concern displayed across his handsome face. She gasped with shock at the sudden arrival of the man. The woman tried hastily to tell the man what the matter was but she could not speak. Her hysterical screams and running had caused her difficulty breathing and she could not get out the words. She simply grabbed the man's hand and led him back along the cobbled street. The gentleman did not speak as he was whisked along the deserted street, his perfectly polished shoes clattering along the cobbles as he took large strides to keep up with the woman's slow running.

The frost was beginning to set onto the cobblestoned road and the small windows that lined along the street began to sparkle in the moonlight. The small street was not very wide and got narrower still the further they ran along. Coming towards the end she pointed down a small passage between two buildings. A street sign named the alley as Tate Hill. The man paused; he knew that this minor passage lead straight onto a small beach, and a dead end. What horrors was he about to be faced with?

The man made his way down the passage; and wearily peered his head around the corner towards the small sandy beach, before he fully emerged into the open. The beach looked deserted and he slowly made his way along the sand. The beach sparkled in the moonlight, as if tiny diamonds were spread along the ground, leading down to the edge of the water, which was unnaturally calm for early February.

The tall man looked to his left. Whitby harbour was in darkness; the street lights had not been lit for weeks. Nobody had been seen after dark for such long time.

Suddenly the man spotted the outline of a woman lying motionless by the water's edge. He ran to her side and immediately saw the horrific injuries that lay upon her. Her elegant dress was torn in numerous places; it was dirty and had small splatters of blood around the shoulders. The woman, who was clearly no older than 20, had severe bruises on her neck and arms; her hair was wet as the gentle tide crashed over it.

The man jumped unexpectedly as a hand grabbed his shoulder. It was the hysterical woman who had finally caught her breath and was able to talk.

'Do you know this woman?' he asked calmly.

'She is called Mae, or at least that's what we all knew her as,' the woman replied, her voice trembling with fear as her eyes scanned the deserted beach.

'What do you mean by, that's what we knew her as?' the gentleman quizzed. 'Is she not from around here?'

The woman looked uneasy; she clearly did not know how to respond to this question.

'Well you see sir… she is a streetwalker; although she hasn't been around that long, so nobody really got to know her.' She stopped abruptly and looked at the gentleman with wide guilty eyes. The tall man could tell that the women he spoke to was also a street walker, and in the current situation decided against questioning her any further on the matter.

Turning his attention back to the woman who lay on the ground he noticed something in her mouth, peeking between her lips. Gently the man removed the item to take a better look. It was a card, the size of a regular playing card. On the back it showed the silhouette of a large black dog, and on the front it displayed only one letter: D. It was painted on in a dark thick red liquid. Blood.

'Oh no!' the man said out loud. 'Not again'. The fragile woman appeared at his side to see what he had found. Upon seeing the item her eyes widened and she looked at the man with horror. A moments' silence passed as they looked at one and other, both unsure what to say next.

'I thought you had caught this man, Detective,' the woman hissed with pain in her voice.

'I thought you were saying only this morning to the Gazette that the man responsible for these crimes was sat in your custody?'

The tall man froze and could not speak; he just gazed at the card with a puzzled look on his face.

'Well,' demanded the woman, 'what is happening here Detective Matthews?' She gave him a sharp probe with her finger.

Detective Matthews blinked harshly as he moved his stare from the card to look at the woman, her face filled with anticipation.

'Well, Detective?' she asked again, looking angrier as she waited for a response.

The detective inhaled loudly and returned his gaze to the woman lying on the ground before him, avoiding eye contact with the woman with whom he spoke.

'I think my dear; I have arrested the wrong man.'

Victoria

# CHAPTER I

## SATURDAY 10TH FEBRUARY 1900

I couldn't help being so angry. All this time he had told me that we were going away for a romantic week away, a belated honeymoon he had said, and now as we are minutes away from pulling into the station he tells me how he has arranged to meet up with his old mentor, now council chairman of the town, and has agreed to sit in on a selection of meetings. I knew he would do this, for this is the reason why our honeymoon has been postponed four times already. This is also the reason he hadn't told me until now; he knows I would probably have refused to come.

I knew perfectly well what lay ahead before I married him. After all you can't marry a politician who is running for Lord Mayor of London and not expect him to attend many meetings during his campaign. It has been his dream longer than I have known him, and who am I to stand in the way of that dream? But still, I would have loved our week away to have been for just the two of us.

The journey north had been miserable the entire way. Dark grey rain clouds hovered over us like vultures in the sky, yet no rain fell upon us as the train bustled through the English countryside. Our train left London mid-morning, and we changed in York to a smaller train. I did not get to see York as we passed through; although I was able see the top of the minster over the small buildings. It stood much taller than any other building and looked beautiful against the dark cloud filled sky. I must remember to visit one day.

I am originally from Somerset, and only moved to London three years ago; thus far London had been the furthest north I had ever been. I enjoyed travelling up the country and taking in the scenery. My sister had even bought me a map of the British Isles so I could see how far I was travelling, and regardless of the distance I was still surprised as to quite how long it took.

When we finally pulled in to Whitby train station I was exhausted, it was now completely dark outside in spite of it being barely 6 o'clock. I hated the dark evenings of winter and longed for the warmth of spring to burst back into life. Spring had always been my favourite season; I loved how it turned the harshness of winter around to reveal the beauty and colour that had been missing from the world; just when you think that it could never look as beautiful again.

Whitby was the end of the line, yet very few people seemed to emerge from the other carriages of the train. The platform was full of smoke coming from the large steam engine still throwing out white puffs of cloud; yet through the smoke I could see that not only was the platform quiet, but the entire train station seemed to be uninhabited. Surely these places do not shut down so early? Where were the conductors? The passengers waiting to board the train back to York? And where were the porters to help carry our luggage?

In the end my husband, Albert, carried our cases out of the station. He held them with such ease, as though they were filled with nothing more than cotton, his muscular arms taking the brunt of the weight. Whitby station was only small, yet despite this the lack of people made it feel like we had wandered into an abandoned old station. The only train pulled in was the one we had just dismounted, the only people walking along the platform were Albert and I; even the driver had stayed at his post as though eager to get back as soon as possible.

As we exited the station I was shocked to see that the streets were also quiet, barely a soul could be seen. The sea fog was also beginning to creep in which did not help. We were desperate to find our accommodation before it got too late.

Suddenly I was startled by the voice of a young boy. I did not hear him approach us in the cold deserted street.

'Would you like me to take your luggage, Sir, Madam?'

The skinny boy must have been barely eight years old. He was certainly not dressed for the cold night ahead, with his ripped dirty trousers that could have been mistaken for shorts and the smallest grey shirt which he had clearly been wearing for a very long time;

it must have been at least two sizes too small. His feet were covered in what took the shape of shoes, but were barely held together with a piece of string. He looked up at me as though I was strange to him; he seemed intrigued by what I was wearing - a long amber day dress that brushed the floor, with mid sleeves that had beautiful lace patterns along the edge as well as around the neckline. Yet it was my large brimmed hat with pheasant feather that seemed to intrigue the young boy the most; had he never seen a lady wearing such a hat?

The young boy turned and gestured towards a horse and carriage parked at the road side. We followed his lead and Albert helped the young boy place our luggage onto the rear of the carriage. The boy then turned and opened the side door and offered me his hand in gesture of helping me inside. I could have cried there and then. This polite young boy was so charming and adorable, his face was innocent and helpless yet his eyes told a story of hardship and maturity beyond his years. His large smile told me that he was more than happy to be helping. I took his dirty hand gladly and allowed him to help me into the carriage. Once Albert had joined me the young boy closed the door, securing it behind us, and climbed up to the front where he could take the reins and guide the two enormous black stallions along the darkened road. A small candle lantern attached to the front of the carriage was our only source of light.

The young boy had told Albert that he knew exactly where we were staying, as the inn's landlord had purposely sent him to collect us. As we set off along the cobbled road I began to search through Albert's jacket pockets.

'What are you looking for?' Albert asked, his voice hushed so as not to be heard by the young boy. I told Albert how I wanted to find some money to give the boy. At first Albert did not look too pleased about this, but I soon convinced him it was the right thing to do.

The streets of Whitby were dark; why were there no street lamps lit this evening? As we got further from the station the fog was beginning to get thicker; I was now struggling to see in which direction we were going. After only a couple of minutes we were crossing a bridge. I had looked up everything I could find about Whitby before we left home, so I was positive this must be the River Esk. I was disappointed not to be able to see anything: I had been reading that Whitby was one of the largest fishing towns in England, and strangely I was looking forward to seeing the harbour and all the boats which lined the river.

Only a short distance from the bridge we took a left turn, down a much narrower street that could clearly only handle one passing carriage at a time. The cobbles seemed to be more uneven, and the young boy slowed the horses in recognition of this. I was just able to make out the name on the corner building: Church Street.

It wasn't long before we had stopped outside an inn. I hadn't known where we were staying; Albert had made all the arrangements for the trip as normal, and I knew it would be somewhere nice. I didn't like when he booked large expensive hotels, and much preferred smaller cosier inns. Thankfully Albert knew this and would always try to find the quaintest place possible on our trips.

As I emerged from the small carriage I found myself immediately at the doorway of a very slender building. A faint light was coming from the window, and the large wooden door that faced me had clearly seen better days. Surely this was not the right place.

Albert followed the young boy through the door, helping to take the luggage inside. I waited in the doorway for a moment for the boy to return, and as soon as he did I thanked him for our ride and wished him a good night; handing over the tip before he left. His face instantly lit up when he saw the amount in which I had given.

'I cannot accept this ma'am.' The boy's voice trembled, his breath becoming visible in the cold night air as he spoke.

'I will not have it any other way, please see this as a thank you for looking after us and seeing we found our way here this evening.' My own voice was slightly shaky too; the slight breeze flowing down the narrow street was beginning to send shivers through me. The frail boy did not seem to notice the cold and extended his hand in gesture to shake my own.

'Thank you ever so much, Madam.' His smile was warm and gentle. 'I'm Tom by the way, you'll see me around I imagine. I hope you enjoy your stay in Whitby, Ma'am, and g-night to you both.'

Young Tom turned back to his horses and taking hold of the reins, he began to lead them along the street. I found myself watching him for a couple of seconds and it wasn't long before they disappeared around a corner out of sight, yet I could still hear the distant sound of the horses hooves clapping against the ground, the only sound to be heard in the darkness. I already hoped I would see him again.

At that moment I caught something moving from the corner of my eye. It was a man, but I could not make out any of his features through the darkness. His face was shadowed by the rim of his top hat as he leaned against the corner of a building opposite but I was certain he was looking straight at me.

Suddenly a hand grabbed my arm and I let out a scream, which echoed up the street. I turned briskly around to see Albert standing beside me.

'Are you coming inside?' His voice deep and serious, yet his face looked concerned at the thought of frightening me. He let go of my arm and led the way inside. I briefly looked back up the street for the shadowed man, but he had gone.

As I entered the inn I noticed the name on the doorframe: 'The White Horse and Griffin'.

D.

# CHAPTER 2

I don't know why I felt the need to go to the train station that evening. It is very rare I would go near that place, it is usually so busy, yet today something was telling me to be there.

It is not the season for tourists so trains are scarce these days, and with all the talk of murders in the newspaper lately I do not blame people for staying away.

I watched as the 6 o'clock train entered the station. It was a couple of minutes early; a beaten up old steam train which had seen better days. It rolled into the quiet station, its brakes hissing and the wheels screeching as the gigantic engine and carriages came to a halt. Smoke filled the platform instantly and as I watched from the doorway I became curious to see if anybody was getting out. That is when I saw her.

She emerged from the train with what must be her husband, a strange looking man if you ask me. They seemed an odd couple. She was extremely beautiful, with her pale radiant complexion set against the amber dress and enormous hat. I could not take my eyes off her and watched as she followed her husband along the platform towards the exit, towards me. I managed to watch her every move as she left the station without her seeing me, her ape of a husband leading the way. It was clear just to look at them both that they were from London. Their expensive clothing and luggage screamed 'Aristocrat' and the way she held herself as she walked was certainly more highbrow than anybody I had ever seen.

I saw them talking to Tom, the young boy who always seemed to find work taxiing people around the town; he never makes much money but for a homeless youngster he always seems to be doing good for himself. The whole town knows Tom, he is always smiling and always busy earning a living.

I watched as they both climbed into Tom's carriage and found myself strangely intrigued to know where they were staying. Before the horses and carriage had time to move I emerged from the station doorway and ran to catch up with them. Holding onto the rear of the cart I perched myself on the back foot stool and hiked a lift with the unaware passengers. As I held on I could hear them talking quietly from within the carriage, her softly spoken southern accent sounded as perfect and graceful as her beautiful face. I tried to hear what she was saying but her hushed tone was difficult to make out full sentences.

I noticed that I was perched next to their luggage, a small monogram atop of each bag which read 'Mr & Mrs Summers'. Despite the cold evening air the leather-covered luggage felt warm against my hands. I so badly wanted to open the suitcase and take a look inside but as the feeling took hold of me the carriage briskly turned into Church Street and I had to hold on tight before I was thrown off.

I knew Church Street eventually led to a dead end. It continued down to the base of the 199 stairs which lead up to St Mary's Church on the clifftop, and of course the ruins of Whitby Abbey.

I decided to dismount the carriage now, and chose instead to hold back. I was keen to find out exactly where this beautiful young lady was staying, but did not want to be too close where I may have been seen. I watched as the carriage slowed down outside The White Horse and Griffin, a quiet little inn that was very rarely busy. Young Tom bounced off the carriage and opened the door for the beautiful lady to get out; as she stepped into the doorway of the inn I could almost see through the darkness that she was unimpressed by the look of the place.

I could not take my eyes off her; she looked perfect in every way; which caused me to feel dirty and unworthy of even being near her. I watched as her husband disappeared inside and she handed over a tip to Tom. I knew there and then that this lady was special, not like any of the woman you would find round these parts; in fact she did not even seem like the women you would expect to come from London. She smiled at Tom as she spoke to him and shook his dirty hand without batting an eye or looking disgraced as so many would.

As Tom guided his horse away I continued to watch her. Why was she not going inside?

Suddenly she turned her head and looked right at me. I froze. What was I to do? For a split second we stood motionless looking at one another. I could not fully read her expression as she tried to strain her eyes through the darkness at me. Her husband re-emerged from the Inn and startled her; this was my perfect opportunity to move out of her sight.

When I looked back a moment later she was going through the doorway of the Inn.

I knew immediately that I wanted to see her again.

Victoria

# CHAPTER 3

Inside our room I realised just how exhausted I was. The strains of such a long day travelling had finally caught up with me and I was ready for an early night.

Despite the disappointing appearance outside, inside, the inn was beautiful. Our room was surprisingly lovely with a beautiful wooden framed bed which had been dressed in immaculate bed linen. Large dark curtains framed the large window, and a good sized wooden desk and chair sat just below. There was also a little wood burning fire in the corner, already lit and warming the room perfectly for us. I removed my gloves and placed them onto the small circular bedside table and admired the room as Albert placed our luggage onto the bed; there was a large dark wardrobe beside the bed facing the window which I hoped had some hangers for our belongings. We even had our own bathroom, which I was assured is rare in such small towns of the north.

The bedroom was delightful and I was pleased by its warmth and homeliness, especially after walking through the narrow dimly lit old bar downstairs, which still, to my surprise, managed to fit two rather large crystal chandeliers from the ceiling.

I began unpacking our luggage, hanging both my own and Albert's clothes inside the enormous wardrobe; I took off my hat and laid it on the four poster bed. I was pleased to see such a large woollen blanket draped on the end for extra warmth. The bed itself looked extremely comfortable, and I could not wait to curl up under the covers and enjoy a good night's sleep.

Albert sat at the desk nestled perfectly below a small wooden window; he was writing a letter, to whom I was unsure. I knew it was more likely to be business related and I tended to stay out his political affairs.

As I unpacked the remaining items there was a gentle knock on the door. Albert immediately stood from the desk and strode past me to open it; stood on the opposite side of the door was Mr Walker, the inn landlord, a plain looking man; he wore dark trousers, a white shirt and a waistcoat. His thinning hair was combed to one side to attempt hiding the bald spot that was starting to appear. His hair which was black had threads of silver throughout and the perfectly kept moustache that sat above his lip had the same. He must have been about six feet tall, was very slim and had a somewhat pale complexion.

'I am sorry to disturb you, Sir,' came his soft hushed voice from the doorway. I paused for a moment in order to listen. 'A number of the town council members have arrived in the bar downstairs and hoped they would be able to see you.'

'Thank you, Mr Walker,' Albert replied promptly. 'Please inform them that I will be down shortly.'

I heard Mr Walker's footsteps departing as Albert gently shut the door again. I knew what this meant: these small affairs always ended up with the men playing cards and drinking themselves stupid until the early hours, and as always I was left behind. Women, of course, would not be welcomed at such meetings. If I was lucky I would sometimes get to sit in another room with the other wives and knit, whilst talking about baking and other such boring housewifely chores, while the men enjoyed themselves.

Albert kissed me on the cheek as he always did, grabbed his jacket and top hat which he had left draped over the desk and walked briskly out of the room. We had not even been in Whitby an hour and I had already been deserted for some social gathering. I had known this was how our belated honeymoon was going to end up, but I didn't realise it would happen quite this quickly.

Alone in the room and with the luggage finally put away, I decided to write a letter to my mother. I knew she would be worried about me as I very rarely left London unless I was visiting family in Somerset. I sat myself down at the desk and began searching the drawers for something to write on. I quickly found some charming paper in the top drawer and there was a selection of pens.

*Dearest Mother,*

I paused. I was unsure what to put next. I didn't really have anything yet to tell her, all we had done was arrive. I couldn't even tell her the town looked pretty, as it was far too dark to really make out anything from the carriage.

As I sat in the wooden chair, I found myself staring out of the window, down towards the dark street below. Only now had I realised that we were in fact at the front of the building overlooking Church Street. Even from my small view of the street I could tell the fog was getting thicker, I couldn't see a single street lamp lit along the narrow road and the streets remained empty. London is still very busy after dark.

Whitby was beginning to feel like a ghost town. Why were the streets deserted from people and traffic? And the street lamps had been left untouched as though they had been completely forgotten – why? My questions were soon answered.

My eyes suddenly fell upon a copy of the local newspaper, lying on the side of the desk. The date upon it was of the previous day, the headline reading:

*Whitby Still in Darkness.*

I picked up the paper, intrigued as to what the

headline could be referring to. As I unfolded the creased paper a man's photograph became visible beneath the short article, his name printed underneath as Detective Matthews. Intrigued, I began to read the cover story of The Whitby Gazette.

This week marks the sixth consecutive week of Whitby's black out. Gas lamps that line the main streets of the town continue to remain unlit during this time following the deaths of numerous victims around the harbour area.

Last Friday it was reported that a man had been arrested for these brutal attacks. However as we go to print, yet another victim has been found, this time on Tate Hill Sands. After thorough investigation the suspect, who cannot be named for legal reasons, was released.

Detective Matthews has promised the people of Whitby that he is certain to be drawing in on this crazed madman, and that he has every hope to have him in his custody imminently.

In the past six weeks, five women have been found dead at various locations around the town, the first being that of Miss Lucy Jones, 17, one of the town's small number of lamplighters, on the night of 28th December.

Ever since then, the streets of Whitby have laid in darkness, with the remaining lamplighters refusing to walk the streets after dark.

George Harrold of the Whitby Council has urged people to remain at home after sunset, and has asked that should anybody have any information regarding these attacks, that they come forward immediately.

The story continued inside, but I put down the paper after finishing only the front page. There was another knock on the door. I jumped with fright at the sudden noise, I had been sitting in complete silence. It was Mr Walker again, who had kindly brought me some food.

'I took the liberty of bringing you something to eat, Ma'am. Your husband informs me that he intends eating with the gentleman from the Council. If you need anything else please do not hesitate to come downstairs and find me.' With that he laid the tray of food on the desk and politely let himself out.

I inspected the white plate upon which was a chicken leg that was so hot it was steaming, as well as boiled potatoes and vegetables; the silver cutlery had been polished and sparkled in the light, and I was delighted to see a glass of wine also sitting on the tray. It was only now that I realised just how hungry I was, and the plate was soon cleared.

Looking again at the letter I had begun to write, I decided to put it away for another day; I did not wish my mother to be upset at such profligacy.

A small bucket of coal was laid beside the fire to help warm the room for longer. I topped it up with a small shovel full and watched as the small flames engulfed the newly laid coal, watching it happily as though it was a form of amusement. It was so cold outside, and I was pleased to have the warmth of the fire as I began to undress for bed. The room was already getting pleasantly warmer; I hated the feeling of being cold, especially at night.

I brought over a small candle on a brass holder to the bedside table and was beginning to get myself comfortable in the enormous bed when I realised I had forgotten to close the curtains. I sat for a moment staring at the curtains, pouting at them in the vain hope they would close themselves. After a few seconds I got myself out of bed again and walked round the large bedframe towards the window. I stumbled and tripped as I stubbed my toe on the corner of the bed. I barely touched the large wooden post, but to me the pain was unnerving as my toe began to throb. The floorboards creaked as I stumbled and I let out a small cry of pain.

Finally at the window I took hold of the heavy fabric curtains that were tied to the sides, and as I began pulling them together I saw in the corner of my eye the outline of a man standing in the middle of the empty road. I looked closer to see if I could make out the person's identity, but it was difficult in the darkness.

As I stared at the figure I suddenly could tell that he was looking straight up at me. I froze with fear at who this strange man could be, and before I could firmly close the curtains he raised his hand towards his face. Intrigued at what he was doing I hesitated in closing the curtains, and as I watched him he seemingly tipped the corner of his hat in a greeting that was clearly directed towards me.

I quickly hid myself behind the safety of the curtains and threw myself back towards my bed. Who was this man? Was it the same man I saw earlier? And better still why was he watching me?

Chris Turnbull

Victoria

# CHAPTER 4

## SUNDAY 11TH FEBRUARY 1900

I had barely slept at all that night. I could not get the image of the mysterious man from my mind. When Albert arrived back into the room at some Godforsaken hour I was pleased to see him. His breath stank of alcohol yet I did not care. As he got into bed I found myself forgetting about my anger with him, and cuddled in close where I immediately felt safe.

We were awoken by Mr Walker around 8 o'clock. His voice gently passed through the door, telling us breakfast was being served in half an hour, before his footsteps echoed back along the landing.

Being Sunday we had already planned on attending church. We regularly went to church back in London, so it only seemed right we should attend in Whitby As an aspiring politician, Albert liked to make sure we attended and were part of the community.

I was keen to get out of the Inn and see the town in daylight. It became clear that there was not much of a view to be had from our window other than the blacksmith shop facing us.

The small dining room where we ate breakfast was at the back of the inn. The only window was a narrow side panel that looked directly into a small courtyard where I saw Tom, the small boy from the previous night, leading one of the large shire horses from the stable and tying him securely to the railings whilst he mucked out. I couldn't help myself watching him; this little boy who was clearly no older than eight must have been freezing. It was another cold morning, a gentle frost had been left behind in the night air, the ground and walls shimmered in the dim light as though they had been showered in sequins, yet I watched the young boy in his ripped short trousers and dirty shirt, dressed as though it were the height of summer; a grey flat cap hiding his unmanaged hair, and large boots protecting his feet from the dirt of the stables. I spent the entire duration of my breakfast watching him in admiration as he went about his chores, oblivious to his audience of one.

Albert was never talkative during breakfast; he would always sit opposite me with a newspaper in one hand and a cup of tea in the other. I would normally be rushing around making sure he had everything he needed for the day ahead. It was rather strange for me to be able to sit down and relax; I was already enjoying this holiday, and it suddenly occurred to me that I also did not have to do the washing up.

Albert has been trying to convince me into getting a maid for months, but I have never understood people that need a maid, for if we had a maid then what was I supposed to do all day. Albert leaves early in the morning and does not return until nearly 6 in the evening most days, for if I had a maid I would only be going round the house after her, helping with the chores, I had never been one to sit down and knit all afternoon..

Mr Walker entered the breakfast room; he was keen to see that we were satisfied with the hospitality so far.

'Good Morning Sir, Madam, I hope you both had a relaxing evening and that your breakfast is satisfactory, and I hope our new waitress is taking good care of you this morning.' He seemed more cheerful this morning, yet his tone was still hushed as he spoke to us. Albert replied that he was extremely happy and told Mr Walker that we had had a comfortable night; I gladly gave a smile of satisfaction in agreement to this. The young girl who had served us, had spent most of her time back in the kitchen, I had noticed her peeking through the small looking glass to see if we were in need of anything, but she seemed happy to leave us be.

After breakfast we got ourselves ready for Church. I had a map of Whitby town spread out on the bed, one my sister had given me, and was trying to see how far it was to the church. I had never been that good at reading maps; most of the time they just look like patterned lines on the paper. My judgment of distance was appalling also, but from looking at the map I was almost certain that we could easily walk to St Mary's Church... at least, so I thought. Before we left Albert checked the map, smirked at me and turned it around. Clearly I had been reading it upside down, but Albert was too polite to poke fun at me. His good-humoured grin was enough to cause me embarrassment and I tried to hold back my own laughter. Albert had a word with Mr Walker on the way out, just to make sure we were in fact headed in the right direction.

Finally out on the street I felt free at last. The fog had lifted and the street was reasonably busy. The smell of the salty sea instantly hit me, and the cold crisp air caused my fingertips to tingle. Children were playing noisily in the street – a group of boys playing with hoops, hitting them with sticks to keep them rolling down the street as they chased after them, racing past Albert and myself in pursuit of them as they gained speed. Further along the cobbled road a group of children were playing with marbles, hitting them against the side of the kerb and screaming and cheering excitably when their friends did well. My sister has two children, I adore spending time with them. Watching children play without a care in the world is so endearing; the innocence and carefree attitude of children I will always envy and admire at the same time.

The street was also filled with large groups of adults, many of which were dressed in their Sunday best – the ladies in beautiful floor-length dresses and their best Sunday hats, the gentlemen in jacket and tie, and most of them wearing hats of a variety of sizes. I could see bowler hats, top hats and even the occasional flat cap and straw hat.

As we continued along I took in my surroundings; the buildings that lined Church Street were all irregularly shaped and were very different in size and appearance. The street was so narrow in places that the buildings would cast deep shadows onto the cobblestoned road below. I was fascinated by all the little shops, and every couple of buildings you would come across another tiny alleyway that snuck between the tightly packed shops and houses.

Half way up Church Street we came to Market Square, in the centre of which was an impressive structure: a stone building that stood out from all the other buildings in the area because of the column posts erected on all sides. The ground floor of the building was open and I could see straight through to the buildings behind. I presumed this was where market traders would set up stalls. Large glass windows dominated the first floor, overlooking the street below, and finally atop the building was a small tower, a beautiful white wooden frame that perfectly mounted the blue and gold clock face upon it.

Without realising it we had become part of a crowd, and everybody was headed in the direction of the church. I took Albert by the hand. I was afraid to lose him in the mass of people; and as we came to the end of the street and turned the final corner I was astonished by the sight before me. Clung to the side of the cliff was what must have been the largest stone staircase I had ever seen, it gripped perfectly against the cliff side as though it had been there forever. I suddenly recalled reading about these steps, 'The 199 Steps' as I believe they are known.

As we approached the bottom step I was astonished at just how vast they were – standing at the bottom I could not see the top as they disappeared around the corner. Edging closer to the first step I figured you could easily fit four, if not five, people across them and still walk up comfortably. Whitby is certainly not as busy as London, yet seeing so many people ascend one stairway was indeed an impressive sight. It was unlike anything I had ever seen before.

We began our climb and before long, I was out of

breath. I was pleased that despite all the steps being different lengths apart, thankfully none were too high; my dress was heavy enough on its own without having to lift it even higher.

Children began to race past us, counting each step as they went, their parents calling after them to slow down. I was pleased to see I was not the only person struggling with the steep incline, as we began to pass people stopping to catch their breath. Along the edges of the steps was a thin black metal handrail that I found very cold to the touch, even through my gloves. Thankfully the morning frost from breakfast had now started to melt and the sky above looked less threatening of rain. At various points along the stairway were what looked like small benches built into the inner railing, all occupied by numerous people catching a breath, we had already passed one or two by this point.

Another passing child raced passed us counting steps, '125, 126, 127…' We still couldn't see the top, but I was thrilled to hear we were past the halfway point; by this stage my legs were beginning to burn with the pressure of climbing. As the steps continued around the cliffside I was increasingly eager to see the top; by now Albert, as well as most of the other gentlemen, was taking two steps per stride. Yet the ladies in their large gowns were forced to take each step in turn. I was now more than ready for a short rest and was thrilled to see a space on an upcoming wooden bench like perch.

'Did you know,' an elderly man perched on the bench spoke less than a second after I had seated; addressing me as though he knew me well, 'these are not seats you know.' He raised his grey bushy eyebrows and nodded his head matter-of-factly.

'Really?' I questioned, genuinely interested in what the elderly gentleman had to say.

'Oh yes my dear, these are not benches, they are for coffins.' I looked at him as though he were mad, and clearly my expression was clear to him also.

'You see,' he continued, 'when the coffin carriers got tired carrying the heavy load, they would place them on these wooden planks while they rested their arms.' I gave the elderly man a smile as he rose to his feet and took off back along the steps. Albert gave me a look that had within it a hidden smile. He laughs at the fact I always seem to get people talking to me, and it is more often than not quite useless topics. Albert finds it highly amusing and teases me, saying it is because I have an innocent face that always looks as though I am interested.

It was now that I finally realised just how high we had climbed. From my perch I could see over the entire town of Whitby. The River Esk below leading out towards the sea was lined with hundreds of fishing boats, and the rooflines of all the buildings were a striking burnt orange colour, each of which displayed large chimneys on top, puffing out grey soot filled clouds from coal fires within. The cliff facing us on the opposite side of the river seemed to be dominated by very large beautiful white washed houses, so grand they looked comparable to those found in London.

The harbour entrance met the open ocean by an enormous double pier, one stretching from the east cliff side of the shore, and the other the west side; these impressive piers with a lighthouse atop of each were very domineering and added grandeur to the harbour entrance.

I could have easily sat and watched Whitby from this angle for hours, and I almost forgot myself if it wasn't for Albert asking me if I was ready to continue.

Every few steps I could not resist looking over my shoulder again at the stunning view. The sea was calm and the noise of the seagulls calling out across the harbour suddenly hit me, and as we reached the top of the 199 stairs I took one last look at the view before turning towards St Mary's Church.

The small church nestled perfectly on the cliff top was indeed very pretty, surrounded by hundreds of gravestones, making it also slightly eluding. Yet the focal point of this scene was not the charming little church, but the breathtaking Abbey sitting quietly in the background. Although now in ruins the structure itself was incredible to look at; I wished I had more time to take a closer look but Albert was dragging me into the church as the service was nearly ready to start.

As we took our seats I soon realised that I was most happy for the rest. The vast 199 steps were indeed impressive, but I did not plan on making climbing them a regular habit.

D.

# Chapter 5

I knew she would go to Sunday service. Just to look at her I could tell she was the kind of person who regularly went to church without ever missing a week, she had a goodness about her that cried out 'innocent do gooder'. She was clearly one not to break the rules.

I rose early to ensure I would catch a glimpse of her. I imagined that even early in the morning, with her hair uncombed and her nightgown on she would still look radiant. I was extremely disappointed when her oaf of a husband was the one to open their bedroom curtains. Thankfully he did not see me staring up at him and he returned his attention back into the room without taking notice of the street below.

I purposely hung around Church Street all morning until I had seen her. I knew roughly the time she would need to leave for church, and right on cue she emerged from the White Horse and Griffin. Her long floral dress came in at her thin waist beautifully; she looked so delicate, like a single flower bursting with colour among the dingy bleak madness on the street.

I watched her from a distance as she took in her new surroundings; she seemed quite taken by the children playing in the street, yet her husband seemingly walked straight past them as though he hadn't noticed them. He walked with authority; with his head held high he took large strides along the road and barely looked at the people he passed – the complete opposite to her. I watched as she took in everybody she passed; walking slower she admired the buildings and the people as if she was seeing life for the first time. It was fascinating to watch her; she was clearly very interested in taking in her surroundings and was enjoying every second of it. Her smile was beautiful and I caught myself smiling too. My desire to learn her name grew evermore; I suspected it to be a name that would complete her beauty seamlessly.

I cautiously followed her all the way to the 199 steps, keeping my distance and blending in behind the growing crowds. It was cold out this morning, and everybody was dressed in their warmest winter clothing. I looked at her in the dress she was wearing; I hoped she wouldn't get cold in the slight coastal breeze.

She marched up the steps at a good speed; many had stopped for a rest more than once by the time she finally decided to stop. By now she was visibly out of breath from the large incline to the top of the cliff. I was already ascending the steps after her, and with some many people also climbing the steps I could not turn back. I could hardly stop and look out of place; she would surely see me. I had no other choice but to continue, looking down at my feet in the hope to pass by undetected. As I passed her, now sitting happily on a seat, she was admiring the views of the harbour below and I was pleased when she didn't notice me as I walked straight past her. My leg brushed against her enormous dress, and I could smell her sweet perfume fill my nostrils with the delight of spring flowers; never have I felt so attracted to a woman in all my days.

As I made my way past her husband, his deep

dominating voice suddenly called out, 'Victoria, are we ready to continue? The service will be over by the time we get to the top.' Her response was vague, and as I continued up the remaining steps I could sense her only a matter of feet behind me, following closely behind.

Victoria, a perfect name for such an amazingly beautiful creature. The name suited her well, a name of beauty and charm. Fate has brought her to me.

At the top of the steps I continued as if to enter the church, but before doing so I briefly glanced over my shoulder to look at her. She had again stopped at the top of the steps to take in the view. I knew this was my opportune moment to skip the church entrance and leave. I knew exactly where she was going to be for the next couple of hours.

Victoria

# CHAPTER 6

My feelings towards the church were changing. I used to enjoying going to Sunday service, especially when growing up as it was the only time I would see my father out of his work clothes, and into something my mother would call 'respectful'. I would find myself laughing as he would always fidget with his shirt collar, complaining that it was far too tight, despite the truth of it being actually quite loose fitting. My sister and I wore matching dresses when we were very young, often made by my mother every couple of months when we had outgrown them. Finally my mother would wear her best dress, the only smart one she owned. I can never recall her wearing any other dress to church during my childhood, which I never gave a second thought of until I was old enough to understand the value of money, and realise that my mother didn't have much. The little money she did have would be spent on new fabric for my sister and myself. Her enjoyment at making us new dresses was plain; yet she would never get anything for herself.

My father owned his own farm, and numerous men from the village would come to work the land. My mother would always be found in the kitchen baking and cooking. Her food was always a delight, a large pot hanging over the open fire could often be seen bubbling away, and the kitchen was always filled with the most enchanting fragrances; the smell of freshly baked bread was one of my personal favourites.

My mother has always loved going to church, but I suspected it was more to do with the fact she got the chance to socialise then with other women from the village. At a young age I didn't really understand. My sister and I would always attend Sunday school whilst my parents attended the main service. I used to feel going to church regularly was part of who I was; but now I was beginning to feel disconnected from it. After all these years I feel as though all I am getting are the same stories told to me over and over again; however, despite these feelings and uncertainties I still consider myself a strong believer.

As I sat in St Mary's church I found my eyes wandering, taking in the beauty of the old building, memories of growing up and my father all rushing through my mind. My father had passed away three years ago this coming spring – how time does pass by in the blink of an eye. It seems like only yesterday I was by his bedside, comforting my mother and sister and trying to stay strong for them both; only to crumble into a hysterical mess the moment the doctor confirmed my father had gone. My eyes began to water as these memories flooded my mind. I managed to catch myself and quickly turned my thoughts to something else.

Being in this unfamiliar church somehow made the service seem fresh and new; for a start seeing different faces was a delight, and my eyes were continuing to admire the quaint building. I was also enjoying the fact that we were miles away from home.

As the service ended and people began to leave I was taken aback by the number of people who wanted to speak to Albert. I knew none of these people yet for some reason they felt the need to shake Albert's hand and formally introduce themselves. I had heard about northern people being very friendly, but I was surprised to see exactly how friendly, smiling and talking to us both as though we had known them a long time.

Descending the 199 steps was a lot easier than climbing; however I still had to be careful not to trip on my dress. As we made our way back along Church Street the crowd of people began to disperse and we were once again back outside the inn. Mr Walker had promised us a hot meal upon our return to the White Horse and Griffin; and as promised the food was ready the instant we stepped though the door. The dining room was layed out exactly as it had been for breakfast, large wooden tables all with fresh white linen tablecloths and a single candle in the centre of each, silver cutlery that sparkled in the candles' glow and wine glasses so pristine they could have easily been mistaken for new. In total there were only eight tables, but we were once again the only couple to enjoy the magnificent open fire in the corner of the room, crackling away and glowing a deep orange warmth that filled the room with an intimate cosy feel. I had barely noticed it this morning, but now as I stared at it I wondered how on earth I could have missed it, after all it dominated the entire wall.

The dinner we had was roast chicken, served with boiled potatoes, vegetables and home made Yorkshire pudding, which I had to admit were the best I had ever tasted. We also received a fruit crumble dessert with a pot of tea to finish. I was full to the brim and had to leave a small amount of pudding; Albert on the other hand never seems to be full and I could even see him eyeing up the remainder of my crumble.

With church over I felt like our holiday was now starting, and my mind began to think about all the things I wanted to see and do whilst in Whitby.

'Would you care for a walk later today maybe, once we have freshened up?' I asked Albert, hoping he would be keen. I wanted to take advantage of the clear fresh air whilst the weather was dry; and of course I wanted to see more of what Whitby had to offer. I was pleased that Albert was fast to agree; he seemed just as keen to take a walk around the town.

'Tomorrow my dear,' he then went on to tell me, 'I

have arranged for a carriage which will take us out to Robin Hood's Bay.' He smiled at me with such conceitedness, as though I was to be flabbergasted by his brilliant idea; the problem was I had no idea where Robin Hood's Bay was, and had certainly never heard of it. But a day trip out, just Albert and I, sounded perfect, wherever we ended up. I had no idea how much business he planned while we were here, so I was certain to take advantage of as much time together as possible.

It was close to 2 o'clock when we finally left the inn for our walk. The sky was again overcast and the streets were a lot quieter than they had been in the morning. Having already walked down Church Street we decided to turn left out of the White Horse and Griffin where we quickly came back onto Bridge Street. Being a Sunday nothing was open, all the shops and businesses were in darkness. It was nice to experience the town in such a way; I imagined that the streets were a different place during the busy working week.

We quickly found ourselves strolling over the Whitby swing bridge, with its large stone built supports coming up from the river bed, that had a metal framed bridge hanging between, the river Esk silently flowed beneath our feet as we crossed the impressive channel. We stopped in the centre of the bridge for a minute or two to take in our surroundings; the river edge was lined with fishing boats of all different shapes and sizes, tightly held to the dock side one behind the other. The salty air left a gritty taste in my mouth and felt fresh as it entered my lungs. The slight breeze coming straight from the open ocean beyond, it felt crisp and pure, even if it did have a subtle odour of seaweed about it. I was in awe looking down the river towards the mouth of the harbour which lead out into the sea: it looked a lot like a portal into another world, the two large piers came together in perfect symmetry, leaving just enough gap to see the turbulent dark ocean beyond, a scary desolate world in which I would hate to be stranded.

We continued walking along to the opposing side of the river, from here I could see St Mary's Church nesting perfectly upon the east cliff, and the colossal 199 steps snaking its way up the side of the cliff, the base of which was hidden behind the tightly packed houses.

As we continued along the harbour I suddenly realised that Albert and I had not spoken a single word to one another since leaving the Inn. True, we were both enjoying taking in the new sights around us, but it was very unusual for him to be this quiet.

'Is everything alright darling?' I asked, rather cautiously as I saw he seemed to have a serious expression upon his face.

'I am sorry, V,' he said softly to me; V was the pet name he called me when we were alone. He would never refer to me as such in front of company.

'I saw you looking at those children playing in the street earlier, and last night when young Tom brought us to the Inn,' he continued. 'I know this is something we have spoken about before, and I think now is the ideal time to start'

I was shocked by his brutal honesty and forwardness towards the subject. He had never been so blunt and I was slightly taken aback by this almost unexpected topic. It would be a year since our marriage next month, and he had casually brought up the topic of children numerous times. I had always given it the cold shoulder and told him that I did not think it to be the right time until after our honeymoon. With the honeymoon being delayed so many times I have managed to keep this conversation at bay, but now I supposed I would have to face it.

'Why are you in such a rush darling, we do not need children right this minute, of course I would like children in the future but right now I was hoping to spend some time just the two of us before we bring another life into the world.' He looked at me as though I was just making excuses, and to be fair I was. The idea of having children I loved, and it was all I had ever wanted, but now the time had arrived, the reality of it scared me senseless. What if I was a bad mother?

'V, we have been married nearly a year and you have been reluctant to talk about such things for all this time. I think we need to start making our plans for the future now and stop worrying about things so much.' He looked at me with hope in his eyes. When he looked at me in this way I knew instantly why I fell in love with him. He was very handsome and tall, not to mention extremely intellectual, I am sure he would have drawn the attention of many young ladies before he met me; yet now as he nears 30 and the small lines begin to show around his eyes, and the slight grey hairs that catch the light; I could see why he didn't want to wait any longer for a child.

We continued walking along the harbourside; a

small number of men were working hard loading and unloading a boat, however being a Sunday I guessed this was probably a quiet day along the harbour in comparison.

We passed numerous hotels, shops and even a library along the harbour front; I knew I would be calling back to the library on one of the days Albert was meeting his old friend. There were also numerous shops especially dedicated to selling fish and chips.

The seagulls flying overhead suddenly become more vocal the further we walked towards the sea, before they had sounded like a distant cry echoing from the cliffs, but as we got closer to the west pier they became more common and loud. They swooped over our heads like giant white eagles, calling to each other in their high pitched calls; never had I seen birds as large as these, and the noise they made screeched along the harbour and filled Whitby's streets with a continuous cry. It was not at all pleasant.

We continued along the west pier, its stone structure was so vast that you would almost forget you were walking upon a pier at all, with small benches lining the centre of the walkway every couple of feet, and between these were traditional gas street lamps. To the left of the pier was a large beach that was slowly being covered by the tide as it drew into shore. The beach was towered by Whitby's west cliffs, a jagged rock face that had clearly been beaten by the North Sea. To our right was the River Esk, finally meeting the open sea for the first time. In direct line with our pier was the east cliff pier, it perfectly mirrored us as it also stood tall and vast above the river below. At the end of each pier stood a lighthouse, as we approached the one on the west pier I was amazed by the sheer scale of it; the shaft of which had a vague resemblance to what I would consider a Roman column, and on top was the cabin which housed the light. I knew I wanted to come back in the nightfall to see it lit up for certain.

I looked back towards the harbour. It looked a lot larger from this angle, and from here I could see St Mary's Church again, it looked quaint and petite however this time as I could also see the magnificent ruins of Whitby abbey standing tall behind, it looked haunting yet magical in the dimming light, it was certainly another place I wanted to visit.

It was beginning to get late, and with the late afternoon breeze picking up we were both starting to feel the cold; taking the same route back to the inn we seemed to get there in no time at all. I knew I wanted to finish my letter to my mother, I wanted to tell her how beautiful Yorkshire was and that she must bring herself and my sister up here one day for a holiday. I could tell it would have been even more beautiful when summer arrived.

D.

# CHAPTER 7

**A**s I lingered around the back of the church I could hear the service start; the organ playing and the echo of voices as the congregation began to sing in unison. It had been years since I had even stepped foot into a church, and I had no intention of changing that today.

I often spent time in the churchyard, however; it was a quiet place for me to be alone with my thoughts. Such solitude was impossible to find on Sundays with such a large amount of people arriving for the service, and so I often found myself retreating away from the cemetery and taking long walks along the clifftops.

Today however I did not want to be away from town, and instead decided to head back to keep a look out for when she... Victoria... got back.

As expected she and her husband arrived back at the inn together. I knew that it was likely dinner would be served for them, but I sensed that she would not want to stay inside the inn for the remainder of the day.

I kept an eye on the inn all afternoon, watching out for her every move, and as predicted she again left the inn for an afternoon stroll. Why was *He* always by her side?

I followed at a careful distance, intrigued simply to watch them; they barely spoke the entire walk. Why?

I was beginning to get impatient and my exasperated need for her touch was causing my blood to boil and my heart to race faster. I began imagining her beautiful hands against my face and the taste of her lips against my own. Watching her walk with that idiot man began to madden me, I knew I would be a much better companion to her than he.

It was beginning to get too much; I watched as they headed back towards the inn and knew I would not get to her now until tomorrow.

I needed to let off some steam.

Chris Turnbull

D.

# CHAPTER 8

## MONDAY 12TH FEBRUARY 1900

I had been wandering the streets for hours now, my legs tiring from constant walking. It was late; I could sense that midnight had already passed. I could feel myself getting ever more irritated as I walked around the empty darkened streets alone, my mind racing faster and faster, yet it was *Her* that I could not stop thinking about.

Fewer and fewer people ventured out after dark these days, even the streetwalkers had not been seen for days, if not weeks; they no longer felt brave enough to walk the silent streets, their business suffering greatly through lack of customers.

I found myself on Church Street once more, and more precisely, I found myself outside the White Horse and Griffin. I looked up at the window I knew she was behind, fast asleep with not a care in the world. It was another bitter cold night.

Suddenly I heard footsteps coming from up ahead, I could tell immediately they were women's from the sound of heels against the cobbled road. I squinted in the darkness to see I saw a woman coming out, locking the door behind her before she continued along towards the market square where she turned left and out of sight.

I quickly pursued her as silently as I could, making sure my steps mimicked her own to hide the sound of my own footsteps and ensure I was not detected. By the time I reached her she was in the middle of the deserted market square.

'Excuse me Miss?' I startled her as she let out a small groan; she turned and looked at me. My tall figure must have been quite alarming for such a tiny woman: she looked to be barely twenty, with her flaming red hair making her instantly recognisable as the barmaid from the Black Horse public house.

'Can I help you?' she asked, her tone cold and dismissive.

'A young lady like you should not be walking in dark streets alone; it is dangerous after all.' She looked at me unimpressed by my remark and quickly turned to continue her journey. 'I am sure I will be alright. Thank you sir for looking out for me; goodnight.'

I had never been spoken to like this before. I found this rather rude and she was clearly unafraid of me. I strode up behind her, my steps were twice the length of hers so it did not take long for me to be directly behind her again. I took hold of her wrist and turned her to face me.

'I told you it is not safe to walk alone, I need to escort you for your own safety.'

She pulled her wrist from my grip and spat 'leave me alone' before turning and running.

I immediately gave chase and again was on her before she had barely made a couple of strides. I pulled her close to me, and held her mouth closed with my other hand. She could not make a noise but her eyes bulged with anger as though screaming on their own; the warmth of her pale skin against my hand was delightful.

I guided her into a small nearby alley – there were always plenty to choose from in the narrow streets of Whitby – and here I uncovered her mouth. She spat in my face and swore at me to let her go. I laughed at this ridiculously feisty woman. Did she really think I would do as she asked when she had the indecency of being so rude?

I placed my free hand upon her left breast. She tried to fight me off but I was too strong for her. I grabbed her by the hair and pulled her face towards my own, our lips met for only a split second; her warm lips against mine was the sensation I yearned for. I began to kiss her neck and she suddenly stopped fighting, as though she realised I was far too strong for her. Yet I somehow believe she enjoyed it.

I began to move my hand under her long skirt. I wanted to feel her beautiful legs against my hand. I knew I could not do this directly for I was already wearing my leather bound gloves. Through them I would be able to feel the warmth coming from her thighs. She began to scream again and the kissing of her neck turned into more of a bite. She began to scream louder and I found myself biting her harder and harder the louder she got. I suddenly felt her skin break under my teeth; I let her go and she fell to the floor with a loud thud, all the while screaming for help. I knew I could not leave her; she had seen my face. I knelt down on the floor directly above her and again placed my hand over her screaming lips to silence her. She instantly began to struggle as though trying to get me off. I could see dark stains of blood trickling down her neck towards the ground. Never had I caused that much blood before. I held her still the best I could and began to lick her neck, the taste of her warm blood against my tongue was delightful, bitter with a hint of copper; I tried to squeeze as much out as possible. Her eyes looking up at me in horror as I covered her mouth once more with my left hand, and a tear slowly fell down her cheek as she stared deeply back into my eyes.

When the blood wound began to slow I raised myself from over her body, still knelt beside her she looked at me silently for a moment, before swearing at me again and screaming.

'Be quiet!' I demanded, but her screams for help loudened. I slapped her across the face in the hope to stop her hysteria, but her screams continued. I held one hand across her mouth and the other against her throat; I needed to silence her before somebody come looking at what the commotion was. As she tried to fight against me, my hand against her throat tightened.

A few minutes later I was walking back up towards Church Street, I again stood outside the White Horse and Griffin and looked up towards the darkened window behind which She slept. I thought I would have quenched my thirst tonight, but standing outside the Inn I felt the desire that took hold of me get stronger; I knew I needed to meet this Victoria alone, one way or another.

Detective Matthews

# CHAPTER 9

I was not feeling the most cheerful this morning to begin with, it had been over a week since I had arrested the wrong man for the murders and I was not only beginning to get hassle from the Whitby Gazette but I was beginning to lose the faith of the town. The chief at the station was also losing patience and I knew that if I didn't start producing facts soon he would replace me on the case, and I was determined not to let that happen.

It was a little after 7 o'clock, and I was getting ready to leave for the office when an almighty banging noise startled me. Somebody was at my front door and they were clearly not going anywhere until I had opened up. I approached the door cautiously; whoever was standing on the opposite side was clearly desperate to be seen. My hand hovered over the gun which perched in its holster, strapped securely around my chest. My hand shook as I reached for the latch; I left on the chain and opened the door only an inch to see who was standing on my front porch. I was directly faced by Constable Taylor, a junior police officer still in his late teens, who had been sent through to Whitby from Scarborough only one or two weeks ago as a potential new partner for me, yet I was slightly reluctant towards the idea of having a partner. He looked all of a fluster as he tried to catch his breath. I released the door latch and invited him inside, but he shook his head abruptly.

'What's the matter man?' I asked sharply, beginning to get impatient with his flapping.

'A woman…has been found in a small alley… just off Sandgate,' he finally managed to say through staggered breaths. Without hesitation I grabbed my coat and hat hanging just beside the door, and followed him out into the street.

On the short walk across town, Taylor explained to me that the woman had been found by a fishmonger, who had arrived early at his shop, and found the young woman in the shadows of the alley running alongside.

'At present nobody has named her and two officers are guarding the entrance to the alley until you arrive, Detective.' Taylor had always shown promise towards becoming a good police officer, his hair was dark brown, almost black, and he was extremely tall and thin, yet his rounded face made him look as if he was twelve years old.

When we arrived at the scene, a number of local business owners had already begun to crowd around the area, trying to take a look down the passage. I pushed my way between the numerous people and nodded towards the officer on guard before entering the alley, Taylor following close behind.

It was still relatively dark outside, so seeing clearly in the shadowed passage was extremely difficult. I knelt to the ground allowing my eyes to adjust to the dimness of the alley, my eyes first found the woman's legs: they were partially uncovered from her dress and small bruises were visible above her knees. As I moved my gaze higher I could see her dress was dirty and slightly torn which indicated to me she had struggled. As I reached her neck I gasped at the sight of dry stained blood covering her entire neckline and chest area. Finally I reached her face, it was pale and difficult to take in as her eyes were still open; yet not a single mark could be seen upon her beautiful face. Her curly auburn hair now fell lifeless against the cold ground; a gentle breeze blew faintly through the alley causing it to flutter.

I recognised the woman immediately; although I did not know her name, I knew she was a barmaid in the Black Horse, so I knew getting an official identification for her should be straightforward. I went to stand, when something caught my eye. Her hand which was limply to her side looked as though it held something within it; I gently prised it open and released the object for which she was holding. I could hear Taylor breathing heavier from behind me, as he closed in to get a better look at my discovery. Lifting up the object so as to see more clearly I was not shocked by what I now held. It was a card, the size of a playing card, on the front of which was the letter D, and on the reverse the silhouette of a large black dog, sketched onto the card in pencil. Another of his calling cards! Why he left it with the victims I could not understand, and why the letter D on the card was written in blood was even more strange and grotesque.

'Taylor,' I ordered, 'I need you to go back to the station and check that arrangements have been made to move the body'. He nodded enthusiastically and quickly headed out of the alley. Before leaving I requested the guarding officer's to stay until this had been done.

I watched as Taylor ran along the street and out of sight, I then turned and headed in the opposite direction towards the Black Horse Inn, where I knew the landlord would be able to help with the identification of the young girl.

As I walked my head began to ache, as my own annoyance at not having been able to stop this attack guilted me, but all I could hope was that something about this latest poor unfortunate would give me the clue to catch the perpetrator of this vile outrage.

Victoria

# CHAPTER 10

**F**or the second day straight we both slept in until after 8am. Normally we would both be up before six, Albert would head off to work early and I would be up making his breakfast. I almost felt lost knowing I didn't have to cook anything, but then I guess that's the pleasure of such breaks.

It was around eleven when we finally left for Robin Hood's Bay; as we headed out of the door we were greeted by Tom, the young boy with the horse and carriage. He was waiting for us directly outside the Inn doors, and his big smile upon seeing us melted my heart. He was such a pleasant young man and always so polite. I had decided to don another floral dress today, with a pink hat to match. Albert as always wore a shirt and jacket and a large top hat that he was very rarely seen without.

The streets of Whitby were alive this morning. Many people graced the streets as shop owners and workers happily went about their business. There was a certain rowdiness about the town today, as numerous wooden carts with deliveries hurtled up the cobbles, some small enough to be pushed by a man, others pulled by horses, their hooves clattering along echoing up the street. The array of people passing by speaking loudly to one another all merged into one loud noise; the general atmosphere seemed good yet I felt as if there was a strangeness about it, as if people were slightly on edge and putting up a front. Perhaps it was me, I wondered, and decided to let it go from my mind.

Young Tom opened the door to the carriage for us and wished us a good morning as we entered the large enclosed cab. A blanket had been laid out on the seat to cover our laps; I quickly took my seat and placed the soft woollen blanket firmly over my knee. Albert, sat beside me, jokingly grabbed the blanket from me to cover his own legs, smirking like a school boy. I playfully slapped his arm and retrieved the blanket, opening it to its full extent and carefully placing it over both our laps. It was a bitter cold morning, and the night frost was still lingering in the shaded areas of the street.

As we set off down Church Street I leaned my head towards the window for a better view, I loved to watch the little houses and shops pass by. I admired Whitby town bursting with people, which now gave the town a new feel to it, like the sleepy town had re-awoken from its slumber. Watching the residents going about their everyday lives was extremely interesting to me; it could not have been any further from my life in London. On the corner of Church Street four elderly women were smoking and laughing as they continued their conversation, all wearing dirty aprons and two of them even had curlers still in their hair. I couldn't help but smile at the scene as they stood cackling with laughter.

As we came to the end of the street I was expecting us to turn right and cross the swing bridge over the River Esk, however instead we continued to bear left, and began leaving Whitby by another route.

The road to Robin Hood's Bay was quiet, and the midday sun made an occasional appearance behind the looming dense clouds above. We did not pass any other towns or villages on our travels, just fields upon fields of moorlands that seemed to roll into the distance as far as the eye could see, and to our left the sea would occasional make an appearance. The greyness of the water met the grey clouds in perfect unison; it was often difficult to tell where the sky ended and the sea begun.

Tom was sitting out on front of the carriage steering the two large horses. He had barely said a single word the entire trip, and if it wasn't for the occasional clicking sounds he made to the horses I would have almost believed he had fallen off the carriage. I found myself worried about him; I hoped he was wrapped up warm against the bitter chill that lingered in the air. It was as if he knew I was thinking about him, as he suddenly called back to us.

'You should see it in summer Ma'am, Sir, them moors are filled with the most beautiful purple heather; that entire view is nothin' but bright purple fields.' After that he went back into silence and did not speak again until we reached the bay. As I looked out of the carriage window I imagined the beauty of the rolling moorland in its grandest colours, and wished I could have seen it bursting with purple bloom.

The journey to Robin Hood's Bay took longer than I had expected. I wouldn't have even realised we had arrived were it not for a small sign attached to a stone mount, advertising that we were entering the village.

We slowly pulled up outside a rather impressive looking building; I could not see the name from my side of the carriage, however Albert's smile as he looked at me gave the sense that something was amusing him. My door was opened by Tom, and he gracefully offered to help me out, and as I exited the cab I gazed up at a large double fronted building. The large bay windows that dominated the ground floor were grand and alluring, on the first floor were another set of identical windows, and above these was a cladded section of the building that nestled smaller windows within. The centre of the building was more modest, with a rather small front doorway that seemed less impressive against the grandeur of the building. There was a further two floors of smaller windows directly above the door. The building looked to be perfectly symmetrical, and the top was finished with three pyramid style points above all three sets of windows, causing a W effect along the roof line. Nestled perfectly between the dipping roofline were two tall stone chimneys, a grand topper for such a magnificent looking structure. Above the ground floor bay windows read two signs, the one to the left window reading *Public Bar,* and the one above the right window reading *Tea Room.* Finally stretching the entire middle section of the building, was the building's name, the Victoria Hotel. I looked at Albert and gave him an amused grin, he knew perfectly well this would entertain me.

We entered through the front door and were immediately greeted by a tall thin man dressed in a waistcoat and shirt, his hair, which was almost completely grey, was combed perfectly to one side in an attempt to hide his balding head, and his half-moon glasses were balanced mid-way along his nose. He barely spoke but showed us through to a table. As we made our way through the main reception I was astonished by the beauty of this grand little place; the wooden staircase circled us along the wall, and the perfectly tilled floor looked as though it had been freshly laid in a Roman temple. As we made our way across the small foyer my eye quickly caught the sparkle from the crystal chandelier that hung effortlessly in the centre of the high ceiling above the small reception desk.

We were led towards the back of the building, and directed to a table in the centre of an enormous set of windows that overlooked the hotel garden, as well as the outstanding views beyond. The garden itself was in perfect condition; again I was disappointed not to have seen it in the summer, as the flowerbeds looked to be home to hundreds of roses, my mother's favourite flower. The garden led directly towards the cliff edge, and came to an end in a V shape, beyond which I suspect a large drop lay down the cliffs to the water below.

On the journey Albert had been telling me little pieces of information about the bay, how it was situated between two cliffs and that most of the houses and buildings lined a narrow road that lead down to the sea. From my window seat I could see numerous rooftops flowing down towards the sea below and into the distance out of sight. It looked exceedingly steep even from this angle.

A girl served us, she must not have been any older

than sixteen, she was very reserved and spoke in a delicate voice when taking our drinks order. Albert had already made the arrangements for a lovely lunch, so after our large pot of tea arrived at the table, we were soon served with a beautiful three tier bone china stand filled with various sandwiches of different flavours, we were also presented with a tray of scones accompanied with jam and cream; I was absolutely delighted. Never had we been out and eaten like this, in fact it was rare we went out to eat at all, and if we did it would normally involve being with colleagues of Albert's. I had noticed a tray of pastries and cakes nestled in the corner of the room, and it didn't take long for me to crave a little sweet treat. I would have to sample at least one; after all, we were on holiday.

We spent the next couple of hours watching the world pass us by; I couldn't take my eyes away from the window, watching out across the vast dark sea as it mirrored perfectly the dark clouds above. Looking out and being so high upon the clifftop, watching the ocean from above and seeing the gulls swoop over the cliff side without a care, you could almost mistake yourself for being at the edge of the world. The wind outside was beginning to rise and the sea below began to look stormy. The dramatic jagged coastline looked haunting yet somehow enticing. I could not tear myself away from the view.

D.

# CHAPTER II

The town has again gone into panic over the latest murder, why do people get themselves into such hysteria over things that do not concern them? I decided to lay low for a while and hope the alarm raging through the town would calm soon. I was in St Mary's Church graveyard when the sun finally rose, lighting up the harbour and tearing away shadows that had once been. It wasn't long before the sleepy town bustled into life before my eyes. I had already watched most of the fishing boats leave, their tiny lights shining up towards the river mouth as they left the harbour and ventured into open water, from where they all headed off in different directions in search for the best spot to catch their desired fish; some even returning before the sun had barely been up an hour.

I did not mean to kill that girl, in fact I never mean to kill them. Why must they scream and cause such a fuss? I am not the monster they claim me to be, I do not wish them any harm. All I desire is the touch of a lady, the feeling of her warm skin and luscious lips. All I crave is for the feelings I have inside of me to be reciprocated.

I sat in the churchyard for some time; it wasn't a place that many people seemed to visit so I knew I would be perfectly at peace here from any strangers. I could see my breath in front of my face as I breathed; a warm mist that mocked me as it disappeared into nothingness.

Occasionally I would walk around the cemetery, for no other reason than to stretch my legs. I had taken to admiring an old sundial mounted onto the side of the church, high above the peasant's doorway. I don't know why I liked it so much, it was easily forgettable and could easily be missed by passers-by. The stone face of the sundial was framed in what looked as though it should have been an old miniature window, it did not have any numbers and seemed weathered as it camouflaged perfectly with the rest of the church wall. The small dial that stood out was thin and rusted, and above this, carved into the stone were the words, "OUR DAYS PASS LIKE A SHADOW".

I continued around the edge of the church and found myself gazing in the direction of the 199 steps. How I longed for her to appear at the top, her face scanning the churchyard for me. But sadly I knew it was never going to happen; she did not even know I existed and I somehow needed to change that. Beside the top of the steps my eyes fell upon a large stone cross. I had walked past this many times and never once looked to see who this impressive monument was for. The cross itself had only been here for a couple of years, and as I drew closer to it I was amazed at the sheer height of it. It must have stood over 12 feet tall, and was carved into various patterns and designs, the most impressive being that of four portraits lining the front, the top one being Christ and the bottom being Cædmon himself holding onto a harp that looked like it was being handed to him by an angel. Below the four carved portraits were the words; "To the glory of God and in memory of Cædmon the father of the English Sacred Song. Fell asleep hard by - 680". I had no idea why this cross became so interesting to me, like the sundial they both blended perfectly into their surroundings and could easily be over looked if one did not stop to take the time to admire them. Could the same be said for a person? For weeks I continue to walk the streets of Whitby and yet nobody seems to notice as I blend into the background.

I returned to my bench and continued my watch over the harbour below. I took out a book that was buried deep within my coat, its yellow bound cover so bright it could have been seen even in the thickest of fogs.

I looked down at it, stroking its spine gently as though it were a pet on my knee. I carry this book with me everywhere I go; like a bible it comforts me and keeps me company when I am alone. I must have read the book a hundred times or more; the pages were already becoming worn and the spine had a small crack emerging. Never have I felt so much admiration towards a piece of literature as this, never have I wanted to delve into the pages and meet the characters, be the characters. Often I daydreamed about it, envisioning myself as the handsome leading man, in search for my beautiful leading lady. I would do anything to be more like him, to have his presence, to dress like him and even mimic him to a certain degree. Yet for all my efforts I am still alone, sat in a graveyard watching as people go about their lives, unaware that I watch them from above.

*HE* would not stand for it. *HE* would demand the attention and affection he deserves.

I continued to stroke the book that remained tightly gripped in my hands, its slight abrasive texture felt warm against my cold finger tips, and as I looked down at it the red letters sprayed along the top stared back at me. Dracula, by Bram Stoker.

## Detective Matthews

# CHAPTER 12

I t was mid-afternoon by the time I left the station; the girl's body had finally been identified as Miss Charlotte Rose, aged nineteen. I had spent nearly an hour listening to her father as he aggressively shouted at me across the police station desk.

'If you were to do your bloody job properly this would never have happened!' he yelled at me, throwing over a number of chairs in his mad outburst. Two officers had to restrain him and escorted him into an interrogation room until he had calmed down. His wife barely said two words; she continually sobbed throughout the entire incident, which said all I needed to know.

Mr and Mrs Rose were eventually escorted home by a senior officer. My heart sunk into my stomach as I watched them leave arm in arm, comforting one and other for their loss.

I was about to fetch my hat from the headstand next to the door when my name was called out from behind me.

'Matthews. Can I see you in my office, please?' It was the superintendent, and he did not look his normal cheery self. I guiltily followed him into his large round office; a large dark wooden desk dominated the grand room, and a large window overlooked the river behind it. I took the only wooden chair available opposite him and waited in silence for what I was expecting to be a lecture. I was not disappointed.

He sat staring at me for a moment before he spoke, clearly unsure where to start. His grey hair and blue eyes were striking, and the subtle lines around his eyes did not reveal his true age, a matter of weeks away from retiring yet he barely looked older than 45.

'Matthews, how long has it been now since the first murder?' His voice was stern, with a tone that told me that he was in a foul mood. I could also tell by his expression that he knew exactly how long it had been and merely wanted to emphasise it to me. I gulped hard and avoided his deep stare before finally finding my answer.

'Six weeks, sir,' I replied sheepishly. My superior began to rub his forehead as though soothing an impending headache. Another awkward silence arose as he clearly tried to find the exact words he wanted to say.

'As you are aware Matthews, we are under immense pressure to find this man. As the days go by, and obviously as new victims are discovered, the reputation of this force is under question. Please tell me that you are getting closer to finding this man.' He looked at me through thinned eyes, almost bracing himself for the worst of replies. I placed my head in my hand, covering my eyes which suddenly felt heavy, as though filling with tears, my emotions still high after seeing Mrs Rose sobbing over her daughter's death, and my own guilt twisting at my stomach.

'This leaves me with only one alternative detective.' I raised my head and looked him straight in the eye, bracing myself.

'I am giving you until the end of the week. If you

do not bring me either that blasted man in handcuffs, or evidence so substantial that will move the case on faster, I am afraid I will have to replace you on this case.' My heart skipped a beat, my stomach sank and suddenly I felt physically sick. Never in my twenty years in the police force had I ever been replaced or removed from a case. My expression must have been obvious as the chief's voice suddenly softened slightly.

'Matthews, you are a good detective, but this is no longer about you or me anymore, this is about finding this monster and stopping him before more deaths occur. I do not want to retire knowing this is how things are left behind; now get out and do the damn job and get me some results now.' I did not reply, but shook my head in acceptance of what he had said.

'Go home detective. Get some rest and see tomorrow as a new start, see it with different eyes and above all get yourself seen out there.' He did not wait for me to say anything and waved me out of his office. I did not need to be told a second time and immediately left.

The walk home seemed to take longer than normal, my mind racing with the events of the day. Once home I lit a fire; the house had grown very cold and the evening was drawing in. Sitting in my kitchen my mind was fixated on the blood stained card which I found in Charlotte's hand, the letter D vivid in my mind. I now had a deadline, an end point that would either see me removed from the case, or the killer brought to justice. In six weeks I had shamefully come up with nothing; I wasn't counting my chances of success in just four more days.

Victoria

# CHAPTER 13

**B**y the time we returned to Whitby it was already late afternoon. I was again looking out of the carriage window taking in the delights of the town as it got closer into view. Coming over the moors the town looked charming in the valley below; it appeared small yet tightly packed together. It was so beautiful and unique; I wanted to make sure I never forgot this place.

Entering the centre of town there were still a lot of people going about their daily business; however now the strange atmosphere I thought I had felt earlier was more abundant than ever. People were barely speaking or looking at each other and kept themselves to themselves. Had something happened, or was it just that the people I saw now did not know one and other?

'There is a rather strange feeling in town this afternoon.' Albert broke the silence, his words mimicking my own train of thoughts. I looked at him to acknowledge his comment, nodding in agreement before turning to look back out the carriage window.

We pulled up outside the White Horse and Griffin and as always young Tom was there to open my door, his adorable little face smiling up at me. He took hold of my hand and escorted me out of the carriage; he seemed to enjoy doing this for me. I handed him some small coins which I had already taken from Albert's wallet. Seeing his face light up with pleasure over such a small gesture nearly made me cry. This boy had nothing and I knew that even the smallest of tips would have been a fortune to him. If God were to ever bless me with a son I hoped he would be as charming, polite and handsome as young Tom. I watched him for a second as he returned to his horses, patting them proudly and talking to them before leading them away.

We had been through the front door less than a

minute when Mr Walker the landlord appeared.

'Good afternoon Sir, Madam, I trust Master Tom took good care of you today and your visit to the Bay was satisfactory?' He smiled and shook Albert's hand as he always did.

'We had a splendid time, didn't we darling, and Tom is a pure gentleman in the making.' Albert always had a way with words. He could please anybody with his intellectual charm mixed with a cool brush of confidence, he was also the kind of man that everybody felt they could trust.

As we turned towards the stairwell Mr Walker's facial expression changed into a more serious and concerned outlook.

'May I have a word with you Mr Summers, privately?' He looked at me as though he did not mean to cause offence. Albert quickly gave me a kiss on the cheek and told me that he would follow me shortly. I was used to this kind of behaviour and headed for the staircase.

It was another half an hour before Albert finally entered our room, in which time I had freshened up and changed into something less floral. Albert found me sitting at the desk looking out upon the street below; nothing particular was happening, but I had developed a love of watching people of all different walks of life going about their business.

Albert did not look in the best of moods when he entered the room, I tried to ask if everything was alright but he seemed reluctant to discuss anything with me. I knew better than to push asking so I changed the subject.

'Do you know what is being served for dinner this evening?' It was only just approaching 4 o'clock but I was already beginning to feel hungry. The sandwiches and scones at the Victoria Hotel seemed such a long time ago already and the cold journey back to Whitby had me longing for something warm.

'I have asked Mr Walker if we can eat early this evening as I have been requested to attend a meeting with some of the town council members at 6 o'clock.' His casual attitude towards dropping that piece of information into conversation was almost laughable. I had no idea about the meeting until now yet I expected Albert would have known for some time.

'Is that what Mr Walker wanted to speak to you about?' I asked. I thought this was a good opportunity to push my luck a little. Albert paused and looked at me with caution. He knew I wanted to know and he also knew that I was smarter than to fall for any of his excuses.

Albert began to undress; he too wanted to freshen up before dinner and change his clothing. At home we would rarely change in front of each other, however in the restrictions of the hotel room we didn't have much choice. I did not mind though, Albert had a good body, he was muscular and had broad shoulders, his arms were strong and his chest had just the right amount of hair not to be considered too much.

As Albert escaped to the bathroom my mind returned to food. We would normally have eaten around 6, but due to Albert's meeting we were now due to eat at half past four. Whilst Albert finished getting ready he finally told me what Mr Walker had spoken to him about.

'A girl has been found dead this morning around the corner from the Inn. My old friend on the Whitby council has asked me to sit in on this evenings meeting; I am unsure why, but I don't feel I can refuse.' Albert didn't linger on this conversation for long, and swiftly moved onto another topic. I couldn't help my thoughts wander back to the subject however. I could only imagine the horror the young girl must have faced.

'I will try not to be too late back, V, but stay indoors after dark for safety.' He again kissed me, but this time, in the privacy of our room it was more passionately on the lips. His strong arms held me to his chest. He knew I would be upset about him leaving me.

Dinner was over as quickly as it had begun. Albert was clearly eager to get away, and with a lack of other people in the small dining area our food arrived promptly. I was starting to wonder if any other guests were currently staying at the inn. I was still enjoying the delights of not cooking or cleaning, in fact I was beginning to think that more holidays should be considered.

Albert left the White Horse and Griffin shortly after half past five; he assured me that he would be no more than a couple of hours before kissing my cheek and leaving. I hated to think it, but I did not believe him for a second; Albert has always been bad with time keeping, especially when it comes to social events. I knew not to worry, and that I would probably be tucked up in bed by the time he got back.

I was not alone in our room long when a gentle knock could be heard from the bedroom door. I called out to enquire who it was and was pleased when Mr Walker announced himself. I opened the door to see him holding a large silver tray, upon which were a large pot of tea and a beautiful bone china cup. Albert had been in such a rush to leave that I decided to request my tea in our room instead. I stood to one side, allowing him to enter the room; he did not stay long, simply placing the tray upon the desk before politely excusing himself.

'I hope this is satisfactory for you madam.' He always spoke with such matter of fact, as though trying his best to please us. I nodded and thanked him for his kindness.

'If you require anything further this evening Mrs Summers then please feel free to come downstairs and see me; if I am not at the bar than there is a small bell upon the counter that I can hear from my office.' With that he gracefully bowed his head to gesture his farewell and left the room.

As well as a pot of tea there was also a small plate of Carr's cracker biscuits as well as a generous helping of cheese. I had not requested these, but I was thrilled to see them. I drank the tea quite quickly, and whilst doing so I continued to watch from the window, as people begin to head home as the shops were getting ready to close for the night.

I suddenly remembered the library which I had seen whilst walking with Albert the day before. I had not brought a book of my own to Whitby but if I was going to be left numerous times whilst he attended meetings then maybe I should get one, I could return it before leaving at the end of the week.

I had no idea what time the library closed, I presumed six o'clock, but I could not be sure. Looking at the clock positioned on the wall above the small fire surround in my room I could see it was already five forty. I had twenty minutes to get myself to the library and choose a book. I didn't think this impossible. I grabbed a hat from the wardrobe and rushed down the narrow staircase into the bar area; as always the bar was deserted and Mr Walker was indeed nowhere to be seen. I hesitated. Should I ring the bell and inform Mr Walker that I was leaving, or even ask him if the library would be open? I caught sight of the clock on the wall behind the bar I could see I was already running out of time. It was approaching quarter to six so I did not have any time to lose. I dashed for the door and burst back onto the cold street.

I walked briskly to the end of the road and in the direction of the swing bridge, I wanted so much to stop in the middle and admire the beautiful harbour that surrounded me, but I knew I did not have the time, I continued to walk as fast as I could; my breath a visible mist before me in the bitter cold evening air. My fingers were already beginning to feel numb as the gentle breeze coming from the sea nipped at my fingertips; I would normally have put on my gloves.

I made it to the library with ten minutes to spare, a large sign upon the door read:

*Opening Times 9am – 6pm*

I hurried inside swiftly so as not to waste any more time; it was already nearly dark outside.

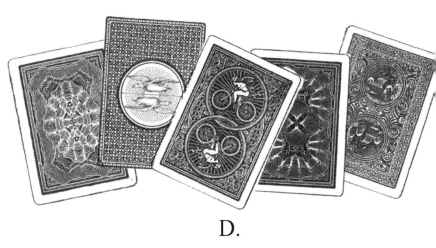

D.

# CHAPTER 14

I had spent most of the day away from the town centre. I usually stayed away for a couple of days after a kill, but knowing Victoria was somewhere among the crowd, exploring the town drew me to come back sooner. It was early evening when I made my way back, although I knew at this late hour Victoria would be back inside the protection of the inn.

There was still a strange atmosphere running through the town. It was always the case when a murder had been reported. News always spreads fast through the small town. The town turns to whispers, people gossiping about the events of the previous night and speculations are thrown around by those who believe they know the truth. As I continued through a narrow alleyway I caught a snippet of a conversation between two laundry women; talking openly and clearly not worried as to whom may hear them in their loud abrasive tones.

'He is losing the respect of the town if you ask me,' the first woman stated, her voice matter of fact.

'Detective Matthews can only do the best he can, I am sure he is doing everything within his power to catch this man,' the second woman spoke in defence.

'Well if you ask me my dear, Matthews has blood on his hands, this crazed man has been on the loose long enough and it is time the police try harder and stop this madness.'

'I'm sure the police force is more than aware they need to act fast, Gladys, but it's not a normal investigation after all now is it,' The second woman tried to argue the case, yet her tone sounded very much like she agreed with her friend.

'Either way Maude, this needs to be resolved fast, before people start leaving Whitby for good. I for one do not want to stay around knowing my daughter is in danger from a crazed lunatic on the loose.'

I had heard enough and dashed through the shadowed alley. Is this really what people thought of me? A crazed man? A lunatic on the loose? They did not know the first thing about me. I was pleased however, to hear that Detective Matthews was no longer the golden boy of Whitby he once was.

I didn't even continue along Church Street to the White Horse and Griffin, and instead cut down through market square, down another lean alley and found myself by the waterside of the harbour, nestled between the buildings. I knew I wouldn't be disturbed here, and hid myself in the shadows as I watched the numerous fishing boats opposite reloading their boats ready for the morning. It was then that I unexpectedly saw Victoria again; she was marching across the swing bridge at full speed. Her face serious as though determined to get someplace urgently, no longer admiring or taking in her surroundings as she once had. I watched her carefully to see which way she turned at the end of the bridge; as soon I saw her turn right along the harbour's edge, in the direction of the West pier, I swiftly retreated back between the buildings and dashed along Sandgate towards Bridge Street. I was determined to get her back into view again as quickly as possible. As I reached the bridge I saw her continue walking against the harbour's edge, I knew I could not get too close at this time but I made sure I kept up with her pace, she was still quite a distance in front of me and I was determined not to lose her. How had she managed to leave the inn without her husband, and at this late hour?

Halfway along the street was a large bend. As Victoria disappeared around the corner I found myself speeding up to ensure that she didn't stay out of sight for long. I continued to walk briskly along, growing more and more anxious about my finally meeting her. What would I say? What would be my opening line? My stomach began to dance with glee, yet at the same time worry overcame me. My thoughts continued to wander as I turned the corner and froze in shock; as I stood on the street's bend I could now see all the way along the remainder of the street and down towards the pier, but Victoria was nowhere to be seen. How could I have lost her so easily? Where could she have gone? I scanned each shop window in turn as I hurtled down the street, checking all the small openings and passages between buildings. Nothing.

I stood for a moment completely unsure where to turn next. Had she seen me following her?

Victoria

# CHAPTER 15

**U**pon entering the library I was instantly hit by the warmth of an enormous fireplace, it glowed and crackled in front of a charming little seated area, filled with armchairs and other forms of seating. Adjacent to the door was a small desk, not too dissimilar to a hotel reception desk. The lady behind the desk had not seen me walk in at first, and was startled when I spoke.

'Is it possible for me to choose a book before you lock up?' I asked approaching the desk. She began to chuckle as she held a hand against her beating heart.

'Oh my dear, you did make me jump. I don't

expect people to appear at this time of the day.' I apologised for startling her before she introduced herself as Mrs Falcon.

'You have a few minutes my love before I start to lock up.' Her voice reminded me of a school teacher, she pronounced her words in the correct manner, and addressed me as though making sure I understood her clearly. I thanked her, and hurried off into the aisles of books, not really bothering to take notice of the genres I was surrounded by. The books were lined on enormous dark wooden shelves that lined up with hundreds of books per aisle. After glancing at a handful of books I finally chose one titled *The Rise of Silas Lapham,* a novel by an American writer named William Dean Howells, I had never heard of this author but from a quick flick through some pages I could see it was firmly set in America, and I had always enjoyed reading stories which were set in other countries. I knew I didn't have time to search out any more and took it with me back to the desk to check it out.

I thanked Mrs Falcon for her kindness. I realised I had kept her a couple of minutes beyond 6pm, and quickly left so as not to take up any more of her time.

Back onto the now quiet street I felt the silence hit

me as I stood on the harbour side. What were once busy streets had now become desolate and abandoned, and in such a short space of time. The sun had set and the final strands of light were being drained out of the sky. Darkness was again falling over Whitby, and the grey clouds above drained the streets of colour.

As I turned toward the direction of the inn I remembered the old lighthouse at the end of the pier. I had wanted to see it lit up, but from this angle I could not quite see it. I knew Albert would be angry if he knew I was out after dark, but I thought if I was quick that he should never find out.

I walked quickly in the direction of the pier. I didn't want to stay out too long as the evening air was getting bitterly cold again and a dampness in the air suggested rain was not too far away. I did not have the appropriate attire to be going around outside in the cold, and the last thing I needed was to get caught in the rain.

Upon reaching the start of the pier I had a perfect view of the lighthouse which stood proudly at the end, from my spot I could also see the smaller lighthouse perched on the adjacent pier. But to my disappointment the light was not on. I thought this rather odd at first, but realised that maybe I was slightly early; it was not completely dark yet.

I had planned to stand and wait for a couple more minutes, but standing still in the cold only made me colder, so I decided to walk slowly along the pier to keep moving and hopefully keep warm. If the light had not turned on by the time I reached the end I would head straight back. The pier was so much longer than I had remembered; I felt exposed on the vast stone built walkway that lined the mouth of the river. It sat perfectly between the river and sea as though balancing between the two; on one side the river gently flowed by, and on the other the waves crashed against the stone body of the pier below.

I had nearly made it to the lighthouse, and was about to give up hope of seeing the light when suddenly, as if by magic, it surged into life and began to rotate, the beam hitting the town before sending out a large stream of light across the vast dark watery landscape.

I reached the lighthouse and continued the handful of steps more until I reached the pier edge. I watched in fascination as the light above me swooped over the darkened horizon, bouncing off the cliffs and scanning the dark waters beyond. It was like a watery desert, empty and hostile. Standing alone at the end of the pier I felt as though I was the only person in the entire world, and the lighthouse was putting on a magnificent show just for me.

An unexpected sound coming from behind me caused me to jump and brought me back from my own thoughts; and when I turned to look I saw a man standing only a couple of yards away. I struggled to make out any features at first; his long black coat almost resembled a cape and his tall hat placed his face into shadow. I paused; my heart began to beat faster as I started to stutter looking for the words to come. My thoughts feared the worst, and the memory of the man staring up at my window suddenly filled my head. Could this be that man?

He must have seen the terror in my face as he soon broke the silence.

'You should not be alone out here, especially in the dark.' His voice was deep yet there was also a slight hesitation in the way in which he spoke to me.

'I know,' I replied, 'I was just heading back to my lodgings.' I began to walk back along the pier. I had no idea who this man was but I was certainly not going to wait around long enough to find out. I continued to walk and he took a step back allowing me to pass. However my own clumsiness soon showed itself when I tried to walk so fast and tripped over my own dress, landing on the ground with a large thud. The gentleman standing by came to my rescue and helped me back to my feet.

'Are you alright, Miss? Please be careful in the darkness, it is easy to trip and not see the unevenness of the pier.' I smiled and thanked him for helping me from the ground. He guided me to a bench situated in the centre of the walk way, I gladly took the seat where I was able to catch my breath.

'Do not worry.' The man spoke to me with a gentle tone, his voice husky. 'I will not hurt you, but I do think I should escort you back to your Inn; Whitby is not a safe place to be walking in the dark.' He smiled at me, a warm smile that instantly made me feel safe with him. Sitting so close I could now see his face more clearly; his large eyes looked grey in the dim light, and shone every time the lighthouse light passed us. His relaxed smile caused small dimples to appear on his cheeks, and he had a small amount of facial hair that was styled around his chin. He must have been no older than thirty.

We sat on the bench only a couple of minutes, the silence between us not awkward and I almost felt content sitting there watching the beam from the lighthouse hit the town. I looked down at my hands; they were dirty from my fall and small pieces of dirt had stuck to my palms. Seeing this, the man instantly took out a handkerchief from his pocket, offering it to me. I again thanked him and began to wipe the dirt from my hands.

'It is such a shame seeing the beautiful town in such darkness.' I don't really know why I had said this. 'Seeing none of the street lamps on makes the town seem cold and unloved.' I continued as I stared back towards the town. This man must have thought I was a complete idiot, but his response to my comments shocked me completely.

*'There are darknesses in life and there are lights, and you are one of the lights, the light of all lights.'*

I was not sure how to respond to this, it was spoken as though he had not purely thought it up himself; it was almost as if he was quoting something. The words were stiffly spoken as though trying to ensure he was using the correct words. I smiled and made to stand. I knew I needed to return to the Inn soon before Albert returned and realised I was missing. The gentleman also stood and held out his hand towards the direction of the town, a gesture that said, 'After you.'

We continued to walk along the pier back towards town, and although at first we walked in complete silence, I soon found myself talking to him. I explained how I had gone to look at the lighthouse, and that I had been in the library beforehand to choose a book. Our conversation seemed effortless, and we were in nonstop discussion all the way back; even if it was I who was doing most of the talking.

Upon reaching the swing bridge I stopped and looked back down the river where I could just see the magnificent lighthouse shining. We stood for only a moment. I turned to look at the strange man beside me and he too was admiring the beauty of the lighthouse. He turned to look at me, and for a very brief moment we were staring into each other's eyes, the beam from the lighthouse hitting us and snapping us out of the trance we were in.

Never had I looked at another man in all the time I had been with Albert, but there was something about this man standing before me that drew me to him. I just wasn't sure what it was.

'Thank you for walking me safely back,' I said as we continued to walk over the bridge. He did not respond, his face turned serious for a moment as though thinking of what to say next. We approached the corner of Church Street when he finally spoke again. The expression on his face had changed again, and his tone of voice became more with an edge of urgency to it. I felt as though he wanted to make sure I heard him out before our moonlit walk came to an end.

'*Do you believe in destiny?*' His words were abrupt. I looked at him as though unsure of his meaning. He clearly thought I had misheard him as he repeated himself.

'*Do you believe in destiny?... That even the powers of time can be altered for a single purpose? That the luckiest man who walks this earth is the one who finds…True Love?*'

He grasped hold of my hand and looked me straight in the eyes. Again his words sounded stiff and quoted.

'I think it is possible,' I replied. I was beginning to feel uncomfortable and was pleased when we finally reached the White Horse and Griffin.

'Well this is where I am staying. Thank you again for your kind gesture in walking me back.' I drew back my hand from his grip and held it firmly in front of him to gesture a goodbye handshake. He took my small hand gently into his own and raised it to his lips, kissing my hand slowly before releasing it and wishing me a good night.

I turned to head inside the inn and immediately paused, turning back to the man still standing in the doorway.

'I am terribly sorry,' I said with such embarrassment, 'but I did not introduce myself, and even more rude I did not ask for your name.'

The man looked me straight in the eye and smiled and leaned in close to my ear.

'We met as strangers, talked as friends, and now it's back to the way we started, strangers,' he whispered softly, his breath warm against my cold ear. And with that he turned and left, walking back along Church Street and out of sight. Fixated I watched his every footstep as he disappeared around the corner, and out of sight.

I dashed into the bar area of the White Horse and Griffin, again it was empty, Mr Walker was nowhere to be seen. I marched back to my room without being seen and once safely back there I was relieved to see that I too had made it back before Albert; I hadn't expected him back this soon, but being out after dark after promising not to be had me praying he hadn't come back early.

D.

# Chapter 16

I spent quite some time looking for Victoria. How had she disappeared completely? I was only a minute or two behind her. It was getting dark now and my likelihood of finding her again tonight was low. I was about to head back towards the swing bridge when I finally spotted her; she was walking slowly along the pier towards the lighthouse. I watched as the wind blew against her dress, her hair now loosely fallen around her shoulders also danced in the breeze. I couldn't take my eyes off of her as she continued up towards the end of the pier; I was hesitant to follow as I knew the pier was a dead end, and I didn't want her to see me.

As she reached the end of the pier the lighthouse suddenly illuminated. Even from my safe distance I could see she was staring up at it in amazement. She continued to walk towards the lighthouse and was soon out of view again as she walked around the large circular structure. I waited patiently for her to re-emerge from the other side, but she did not. Suddenly fear struck me; had she fallen off the end, or worse, had she jumped? After a few moments of waiting I cautiously began to walk up the pier, hoping that I could take a peek at her up close without being seen myself.

I had barely made it to the lighthouse when I spotted her, and within a second she turned and looked straight at me. I was stunned and my feet froze to the ground. I had no idea what to say. My plans of a perfect opening line had gone out of the window after she had disappeared the first time. I finally broke the silence.

'You should not be along out here, especially in the dark.' My voice cracked slightly as I tried to stay relaxed. Her short reply seemed cold and hesitant; she was clearly nervous of me so I took a step back to show her my intentions were not to harm her. As she hurried past me she fell to the ground. I rushed over to help her to her feet and guided her gently towards a nearby bench. Her perfume filled my nostrils and the warmth of her hand filled me with desire. Through the darkness I could have sworn her face was now flushed with a slight pinkness, embarrassed by her own clumsiness no doubt; yet I still thought she was the most beautiful lady I had ever seen.

As we sat on the bench I handed her my handkerchief to wipe the dirt from her hands. She then spoke in her soft West Country accent, not London as I had originally thought, but still a voice I could happily listen to all day.

'It is such a shame seeing the town in such darkness; seeing none of the street lamps on makes the beautiful town seem cold and unloved.' I would hardly call it beautiful myself, but if this is what she sees as beauty then I will smile in agreement. She looked at me as though expecting a reply; it had been a long time since I had engaged in conversation with another person, and never a lady of her class.

*'There are darknesses in life and there are lights, and you are one of the lights, the light of all lights'* was my reply, a

quote from the book Dracula. I could quote the entire book if asked to; it seemed an appropriate quote for this special moment, although the look on her face afterwards seemed that of confusion. My own mind froze as I waited for her to respond, but she simply gave a smile and stood from the bench ready to walk back. It wasn't long before she was talking again. I didn't really follow a lot of what she was telling me, but just listening to her was enough.

We reached the swing bridge and she stopped abruptly in the middle. At first I thought something might have been wrong, but I soon realised she had stopped to look at the lighthouse again. I stood and looked at it too, but I could not see what was so special about it. Did they not have them in the south? Perhaps this was something new to her.

We again continued, and as we reached Church Street she thanked me for walking her back, the smile on her face telling me that she was grateful for the company. I was sad to know we had come to the end of our short walk together; I needed to say something, but what?

*'Do you believe in destiny? That even the powers of time can be altered for a single purpose? That the luckiest man who walks*

*this earth is the one who finds…True Love?'*

I am not sure why I quoted this particular section of Dracula; yet I felt that I was in love with Victoria but was it appropriate to tell her now? Again she did not seem to understand, and simply replied, 'I think it is possible.' I wanted to kick myself; clearly I needed to be more apparent of my feelings for her.

Before heading inside the inn she tried to introduce herself. I already knew who she was, and I was determined that she was not to know anything about me, or at least not yet. I cut her off from formally introducing herself, as I know she would have expected my own introduction in return. I kissed her gently on the hand and leaned in towards her, whispering in her ear,

'We met as strangers, talked as friends, and now it's back to the way we started, strangers.'

I turned and left her standing in the doorway, but as I turned the corner out of her view I paused. I leaned my body back to where I knew I could see her again and caught the last glimpses of her heading into the inn and out of sight.

I need to think of a better way of claiming her for my own. Victoria is too special and too beautiful to be wasted, and from the way she looked at me tonight I am certain she feels the same way about me.

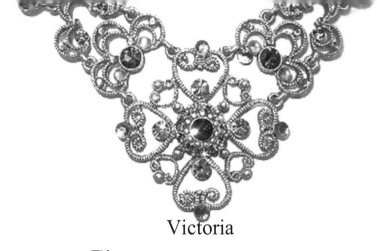

Victoria

# CHAPTER 17

## TUESDAY 13TH FEBRUARY 1900

I had been surprised to see Albert back by 9 o' clock, and when he entered the room I could see straight away that he was in a bad mood, clearly the meeting with the council members had not gone to his satisfaction; yet I knew better than to ask him anything whilst he was still in a foul mood.

Before bed I had myself a bath; Albert informed the innkeeper of our need of warm water and it wasn't long before numerous bowls were being brought up from the kitchen. The big tin bath in the centre of the bathroom was filled in no time. The hot water tingled at my toes as I stepped into the large oval framed bath, my body still cold from my evening walk soon warmed as the water covered my body. After a couple of minutes Albert knocked on the bathroom door and entered. He had come to help me wash my hair, something he had started doing when we first got married which we continued to enjoy, an intimate moment just the two of us. His large hands massaged my head, neck and shoulders as he perched behind me on the edge of the bath still in his best trousers and shirt, I could have fallen asleep there and then I was so relaxed.

Tuesday morning arrived and I had had the best night sleep of my trip so far. The evening sea air must have certainly filled my lungs. I was awoken by the sound of seagulls fighting out on the street below. Whitby seemed to be full of these white oversized pigeons; this morning they seemed more vocal than ever. Albert was still fast asleep. I looked over at the wooden clock that hung on the wall above the small fireplace: it was carved into various forms around the clock face; I could make out a lighthouse, a fishing boat and some fish. It looked as though it should have been a cuckoo clock, but not once had I heard it make a sound, aside from the gentle tick that came from the small pendulum as it rocked slowly back and forth.

It was just after seven thirty. I ever so gently crept out of bed, determined not to wake Albert in my bid towards the bathroom. Being closer to the window I couldn't help but take a peek between the closed curtains. Daylight was already starting to poke its way through the gap and I was keen to see what kind of day was ahead of us.

As I opened the curtain slightly I could see that the grey sky above looked menacing and threatened rain. I looked down, and there, standing alone in the deserted street looking straight back up towards me was the gentleman from last night, his eyes piercing mine as we caught each other's stare. I jumped back from the window and let out a slight gasp in shock. Albert sat up immediately and looked at me, concern spread across his face.

'What is it my dear?' his voice croaky and tired, while his eyes tried to adjust to his surroundings.

'Erm… Nothing, I stubbed my toe on the desk, go back to sleep.' I could tell he was not completely convinced by my excuse, but I could hardly tell him that I walked through Whitby in the dark with a strange man whose name I do not know, and that very same man was now standing outside our window looking up at me, could I?

My heart was beating rapidly; I could feel the blood racing through my body as I tried to calm myself down. Why was this strange man standing outside my bedroom window looking up at me? I peeked out of the window again; I do not know what possessed me to want to look again. He was gone, and the street was empty once more.

When I returned from the bathroom Albert was already out of bed, sifting through the wardrobe for something to wear.

'I forgot to mention, we are going to Mr George Harrold's house this evening, he is hosting a dinner party for us,' Albert declared, his tone of voice casual and relaxed as though telling me the weather outside. I had no idea who Mr Harrold was, although I was sure I had heard his name before. As always I did not question it, I acknowledged Albert's announcement with a simple 'Alright', and continued to get myself dressed.

'What are our plans today before the dinner party?'

I asked casually, hoping that it did not involve more meetings with people, thus leaving me alone.

'Well my dear, it is up to you. Is there anything in particular you would care to do?'

I almost jumped for joy; I was pleased to hear we were spending the day together, even if I had a tedious dinner party to attend later.

'I was hoping we could see the ruins of the old Abbey sometime this week.'

Albert did not respond, but nodded in acceptance and continued to search through the wardrobe. Albert's clothing selection consisted mostly of suits, from day suits to more formal evening attire; he was always well groomed and smartly dressed.

With breakfast eaten, we finally left around ten. I wore my favourite emerald green dress, with sequins around the collar and wrists and a gold thin fabric around my waist with long ties that hung somewhat against the side of the dress. The base of the dress gently brushed against the floor as I walked; my small heeled shoes not quite high enough to raise the dress off the ground.

We walked up Church Street in the direction of the

199 Steps. The street was a lot busier now, the shops were bursting with life and the narrow cobbled street was dressed with an array of people. A group of chimney sweeps walked past, with large brushes over their shoulders, and their faces black as the night covered head to toe in dust and ash; they laughed and joked with one another as they passed us.

As we continued along the street I saw young Tom walking towards us, headed to the inn no doubt.

'Morning Ma'am, Sir,' he said in his usual cheery tone, as he continued past us with a skip in his step. His smile lit up the entire street, as he headed on past and around the back of the inn towards the small courtyard.

I enjoyed looking into the small windows of the various shops as we made our way along the street. Butchers, fishmongers, bakers could be seen a-plenty. There was also a dressmaker that caught my eye, and I was tempted to ask Albert if we could take a look, but I decided I could always visit another day.

Before we turned the bend for the 199 steps, my attention was captured by a large shop with a deep green sign that stretched above two large windows; the sign was the same deep green colour as my dress. It read, 'W.Hamond – The Whitby Jet Shop'. How I had not seen this shop the first time I passed was a surprise to me: the large windows looking out onto the street were filled with numerous displays of jewellery, from the grandest of necklaces, large jewelled rings to the most delicate earrings. All were designed around the same stone, Whitby jet, a black gem-like stone that captivated me as I stared into the large window. I couldn't help but think it looked like small pieces of coal polished up so well that they shined.

I had never been drawn to jewellery. I do like to wear it occasionally but I do not own very much. Yet there was something about the Whitby jet that I liked. It was not a common piece of jewellery, or at least not in London. I know that the Queen wore it; ever since the death of her husband Prince Albert all those years ago, Queen Victoria had been photographed so many times wearing it. Thinking about the Queen always made me think of my sister, and how she would tease me when I first started courting Albert. She would say, 'If you marry Albert then you could be a Queen and Prince stand in for when the real Queen Victoria goes on holiday.' She used to make me laugh with her comments, and she wasn't the only one back then making such remarks.

'Are you ready to continue, darling?' Albert's voice suddenly cut into my thoughts, and I realised that I was still staring at the jewellery through the shop window.

'Sorry,' I muttered, before following Albert around the corner. The stone staircase was quieter than the last time we were here; although I still had to stop halfway to catch my breath. The steep climb of the stone steps was worth it though, just to admire the view back down towards the harbour and the river leading out to the sea was a delight.

At the top of the steps we immediately entered St Mary's graveyard. The small church looked endearing sat upon the cliff edge, surrounded by a vast arrangement of gravestones, all of different shapes and sizes, most of which were now entangled by long grass that had been left to look after itself. From here it was only a short walk to the Abbey; you couldn't miss it towering high in the background. St Mary's wasn't really that small, but compared to the Abbey it looked almost miniature.

The closer we got to the abbey the more beautiful and dominant it became; it was not surrounded by gravestones like St Mary's church, but simply well maintained grass. Besides the wind whistling in my ear and my own footsteps we were in complete silence. The grandeur of the abbey brought goosebumps to my entire body, and an eerie atmosphere could be felt as we got closer still. Despite this I also felt great sadness that such a beautiful building could be allowed to fall into such decay. An abbey as magnificent as this should be standing tall and beautiful, not crumbling into disrepair.

Walking around the ruined Abbey I found myself in awe of it. The roof had long gone and the windows no longer glistered with beautiful stained glass as I imagined it once had; yet despite all this it was still exceptionally beautiful. There was a sense of calming and stillness as I walked around the desolate monastery. As I continued to explore I found myself caressing the cold bare stone walls, imagining how it would have looked, smelt and sounded at the height of its beauty. A gentle breeze caused me to shiver; I did not feel cold yet my body was suddenly trembling. I turned to look at Albert, but he was no longer standing behind me as I had expected. Panic stricken I exited the room which I had only just entered, in the hope Albert was just trailing behind, but he was not in this room either. I was about to call out his name when a sudden noise from behind caused me to jump; as I turned to look I could have sworn I saw a shadow disappear around the corner. Suddenly the image of the strange man standing outside my bedroom window entered my head, my heart began to race and my hands now began to shake. Where on earth was Albert?

D.

# CHAPTER 18

I had been standing on Church Street for some time. The morning light was gradually flooding the town and the sea mist that once lingered along the dark streets was starting to lift. It had certainly been one of the coldest nights for some time. I could not get Victoria from my mind, her voice still perfectly playing in my mind like a phonograph echoing through my heart. The way she had looked at me on the bridge, her eyes soft and dreamy in the hazy light, her smile warm and welcoming. I could tell she was trying to suppress her true feelings; she was married and did not want to disrespect that lawful act and commitment she was bound by. But I knew that if she was to ever be truly happy she would need to follow her heart, and that meant leaving him for me.

It wouldn't be long until Church Street was filled with people once more. I had been standing in a small doorway across from the White Horse and Griffin for some time, unsure what to do with myself. I was shocked when she opened the curtains and looked straight down at me, and by the look upon her face, as she stumbled away from the glass I could tell that she too was shocked by the sight of me. Afraid that she may call her husband I decided to flee, I did not need any more attention drawing to myself.

I headed along Church Street towards the 199 Steps; my destination was St Mary's graveyard. I knew I was safe there from people, and I knew I could sit amongst my own thoughts in piece. Numerous benches lined the cliff top, looking out towards the open ocean, a beautiful scene that changed with every season. I could sit up here for hours, and often did.

I must have fallen asleep, as I was awoken by the sound of voices. Determined not to be seen I kept my head down, carefully trying to peek over the back of the bench for a look at who was around. To my astonishment it was Victoria and her fool of a husband; but what were they doing?

I watched as they followed the pathway behind the church and continue towards the Abbey. However, I did not see her as the kind of person interested in looking at a ruined old building; after all what was there to see really other than bare stone walls that were crumbling to the ground?

I decided to follow them, intrigued as to what they were doing, and watched carefully as they entered the ruin.

I stuck to the outer walls and peered in through the empty windows in the hope of catching a glance of her. Victoria was marching ahead. She looked like a child in a sweet shop, her eyes bright and taking in her surroundings, her husband trailing behind reading an information board at the entrance. Victoria continued to race ahead, clearly excited to see more, leaving Albert by the entrance reading about the Abbey's history. I continued around the outside of the ruin, watching Victoria's every move. She entered a smaller room with a large open fireplace against the wall, where she placed a hand against the cold stone surround, and closed her eyes for a split second; what on earth was she doing?

By now I too had entered the ruin; I could not see her standing beside the fireplace without doing so. As she turned to take in the room she was standing in, I had to quickly crouch behind a wall so as not to be seen. It suddenly went very quiet, I was worried that she had seen me, was I to move or stay where I was?

Suddenly she came running out of the room at full speed, passing straight past me as I crouched in a corner by the doorway, her breathing slightly high. She stopped only yards from me. I was certain she did not know I was there, for surely she would have turned to look at me straightaway?

Quickly I got to my feet and dived through the doorway through which she had only just exited. I did not wait to see if she had spotted me as I climbed through a low-hanging window and swiftly made my way back toward St Mary's graveyard.

Victoria

# Chapter 19

Spooked by the shadow, I ran back in the direction of the abbey's entrance, hoping that Albert would be somewhere to be found. I eventually found him reading a plaque on the wall, his face full of concern as I ran straight into him, almost knocking us both off our feet.

'Slow down!' he exclaimed. 'What's wrong?'

It took me a few moments to catch my breath, Albert held me in his arms to comfort me. My head tucked into Albert's chest, I could hear his heart beating; I was shocked to hear it beating nearly as fast as my own.

'I thought… I had… lost you,' I said through the gasps of breath, 'I'm alright… I just frightened myself,' I lied. 'Let's go… I have seen enough.'

Albert took me by the hand as we exited the abbey and despite the state I was in, I still found myself walking through the doorway wishing that I had seen the grand wooden doors that once stood in the now empty archway.

Albert continued to hold my hand as we walked through St Mary's churchyard, and down the 199 Steps. I tried not to look panicked. I did not want Albert asking too many questions, yet I still found myself looking over my shoulder every couple of footsteps, afraid that this nameless man was going to appear again at any minute.

Once back inside the White Horse and Griffin, my heartbeat had finally reached normal speed, maybe I was just being silly? I couldn't even be certain I saw anybody in the old abbey, perhaps my mind was playing tricks on me.

I told Albert that I wanted to rest for a while, and he left me alone in our bedroom where I intended to have a lie-down, but after a couple of minutes I realised that I was not at all tired. As much as I tried, sleep would not come to me. At that moment I remembered the letter I was planning to write to my mother that I had placed in the top drawer of the desk.

I decided now was the perfect time to finish it, I had now spent a few days in Whitby and had much more to tell her.

*Dearest Mother,*

*Whitby is a delightful little town, you must certainly visit sometime. Father would have loved seeing all the fishing boats that stretch along the harbour, and the sea air is so fresh.*

*Albert has found himself working, and has had a meeting with the local council. Still we have had ample time together to relax and enjoy our visit.*

*We visited a lovely little establishment called the Victoria Hotel in a place called Robin Hood's Bay. It was situated upon a clifftop with the most spectacular views out to sea.*

*This evening we are going to a dinner party at a council members house. I trust it will be a standard affair but I do hope it does not go on into the early hours of the morning as they often do.*

*I look forward to seeing you upon my return.*

*Love you dearly, V x*

Once finished I left our room and headed downstairs to the bar area, I was hoping to find Albert there, but he was nowhere to be seen.

'Can I help you, Mrs Summers?' A voice came from behind me, startling me in the process. It was Mr Walker. 'I do apologize, Mrs Summers; I did not mean to startle you.' He looked genuinely concerned for shocking me.

'I was looking for my husband; do you know where he went?'

'No ma'am, I did not see him leave. May I be of any help?' His voice was soothing and gentle, and he always spoke in a low hushed tone as though trying not to be overheard.

'I was hoping to send off this letter to my mother, but I do not know where the post office is.'

Mr Walker grinned at me, and replied.

'Young Tom is still out there with the horses, if you catch him before he leaves, I'm sure he will be able to take your letter and make sure it is sent off to your mother today.'

I thanked Mr Walker and hurried out of the door, finding Tom brushing down one of the horses. He had not noticed me enter the yard; he was talking quietly to himself, and as I approached I soon realised that he was in fact talking to the horse.

'There y'are boy, nice 'n' clean and ready for yer afternoon nap I'm sure.' He soon spotted me, and he blushed with embarrassment for being caught talking to the large beast.

'Sorry to disturb your work Tom,' I said with a smile spread across my face. 'Mr Walker informed me that you were the best man to see about sending my letter off to my mother.' Tom dropped the horse brush into an empty bucked and strolled over to take the letter, wiping his hands against his trousers to ensure they were not too dirty, before taking it from me.

'That'll be no problem at all Ma'am. I am almost done 'ere anyways, so I'll head straight off and make sure it's on its way today for ya.'

He folded the letter carefully and placed it into his trouser pocket and smiling warmly at me before I turned to leave.

I left the yard content; I knew Tom was trustworthy and that my letter was in good hands.

As I reached the front door of the White Horse and Griffin, I paused and wondered again where Albert had gone. I stood for a moment and looked up the street; it was still full of people, all going about their day noisily, greeting one and other in a cheerful manner. I didn't really want to go back inside the inn, the fresh air was glorious against my skin and the gentle stretch of my legs was strangely comforting.

I decided to walk back towards the dress shop I had seen earlier that morning, and if I had time I may even take another peek at the Whitby Jet shop; they weren't too far from the inn, so I know I wouldn't be away long. Walking along the street I passed countless people, most of whom smiled at me and wished me a good day. I still was not used to such friendliness; never in London would a complete stranger wish me a good day.

I reached the small dress shop and was disappointed to find that they had closed early. I continued up the street towards the Jet shop, I could admire the jewellery from outside the window. I was again mesmerised by the beautiful jewellery displayed. The uniqueness of the jet stood out from other stones and gems, its darkness somehow warming and attractive, yet at the same time with a harshness about it that surrounded it in mystery and intrigue.

I did not go into the shop, through fear of trying something on and wanting to keep it. I must have spent nearly ten minutes admiring the contents of the windows before finally retreating back up the street.

I returned to our room and began reading my book when Albert finally arrived back. He entered the room and instantly took me into his arms, leaning into me for a kiss.

'Did you enjoy your rest darling?' he asked.

'I didn't sleep in the end; I wrote a letter to my mother and came looking for you downstairs.'

'Oh I am sorry,' Albert said, leaning in to kiss me again. 'I thought you would have been asleep so I went for a walk.' He had been gone less than an hour, so I was not angry. Yet being in the room alone had started to become tedious.

This evening we were going to the dinner party about which Albert had informed me this morning. I was not particularly looking forward to it, but let me hasten to say I knew it was expected of me to attend.

We left the White Horse and Griffin just after 6 o'clock; Tom had his horses and carriage ready and waiting for us.

'Evenin' Sir, Madam,' he said as he opened the carriage door for me. 'A bitter wind blows tonight; I hope you will be warmly wrapped for your journey.' He spoke to us with wisdom beyond his years, an old soul within the body of a child. He was right though; a bitter cold breeze gushed along Church Street and caught against my dress. My long black dress with sleeves did nothing to protect me from the cold, and the gloves I wore barely protected my fingers against the harsh bitterness of the evening. I looked down at young Tom, standing there in barely a scrap of clothes, yet he did not seem fazed by the cold at all.

'By the way ma'am,' he said before closing the door, 'your letter was sent off for ya.' I smiled at him in appreciation before he closed the door tightly behind us.

The carriage still had a blanket draped on the seat, which I quickly placed over my knee for extra warmth; Albert took off his scarf and offered it to me, but I politely declined.

It was already nearly dark outside, and the streets were again beginning to empty.

We travelled though the darkness, noticing that still no streetlights were lit, yet as we rode over the small river bridge I could see the masses of sea fog already beginning to make its way into the harbour. The lighthouse's beam lit up the sky above just enough to see where we were headed.

The carriage ride did not seem to take very long, and we travelled in perfect silence the entire journey, as if scared to make a noise in such silent streets. The horses' hooves against the cobbled roads was the only noise to be heard.

We pulled up outside a large row of houses, each of which stood four stories high and three large windows wide. All the houses looked the same, with stone steps leading up to a grand doorway, with a brightly coloured door and a large brass door knocker. Barely a second after Albert knocked on the door, it was opened and we were greeted by an elderly gentleman in a suit. It took my eyes a moment to adjust as the light from the lobby beamed onto the dark front porch. Inside the spacious lobby the man took Albert's coat, hat and scarf, along with my hat to be hung up. The noise from the next room was already overwhelming, an enormous contrast from the silence of the street we had just left behind.

The elderly man ushered us into the room where

we were instantly hit by the heat of the large fire blazing directly opposite, which roared with force inside an enormous open fireplace. The room was a large formal sitting room with a variety of casual seating dotted around the room. I followed Albert closely, and had barely taken two steps into the room when a rather round looking man with an enormous dark greying beard jumped to his feet and greeted Albert as though they were old friends. He then turned his attention to me.

'Ah, Mrs Summers, so pleased to finally meet you.' And the gentleman grasped my hand within his own and continued to kiss it humbly.

'Dear, this is Mr George Harrold of Whitby Council,' Albert quickly interjected, clearly seeing the confusion on my face as to who this man was. 'Mr Harrold was my old mentor during my University studies and worked at Westminster for some time before relocating up north.'

'It is very nice to meet you Mr Harrold.' I stuttered, still a little taken by this sudden affectionate introduction.

'The pleasure is all mine, fine lady,' Mr Harrold hollered, his cheerful voice filling the entire room.

'Please come and let me get you a drink.' And he took me by the arm and led me over to a small table, a large silver tray balanced on top that exhibited a small array of alcoholic beverages. Mr Harrold did not wait to hear what Albert would like and instantly poured him a whiskey, soon followed by a glass of white wine for me.

Mr Harrold then turned and began to introduce everybody in the room. Including myself and Albert there were twelve people in total, and as Mr Harrold introduced them individually I tried my hardest to keep up, I was never good at remembering people's names and as each name was mentioned Mr Harrold also gave me a brief description of what they did. All of the men worked within the council, and all their wives looked just as bored as I was. I was also the youngest of the guests by quite a margin which didn't fill me with confidence for the rest of the evening.

As always with events like these the men would constantly talk about work, while the women sat and politely listened. During dinner I was sat at the large oval shaped table, filled with flowers and a large candelabra at the centre, next to one of the younger women named Alice. She must have been in her early thirties and began telling me that they had hired a new nanny.

'It is the first time she had been left alone you see,' Alice told me, her voice high pitched and girlish. 'I was in two minds whether or not to come this evening, as she is rather young.' I had no idea how to respond to this, not having a child myself I felt myself slightly unqualified to have an opinion, yet the idea of having a Nanny when you are home all day seemed rather odd to me. My mother could never afford a Nanny and raised my sister and me herself, so I had never experienced the effects of such person.

Alice continued talking to me about her children, five in total; the youngest being a little boy named Alfie who was turning one year old next month. I realised that Alice was a lot younger than most of the other women around the table, and despite her being nearly ten years older than myself, she must have been happy to have somebody within the group closer to her own age. Her husband did not speak much.

I could not have been happier when dinner was finally over. Despite there being so many people sat around the table, it was Mr Harrold who could be heard above everybody else with his loud voice and even louder laugh. I imagined he could be heard in the next street. He spoke mostly of his work, but occasionally ventured onto other topics. His favourite seemed to be when he told Albert about Whitby's whaling history and how he was descended from generations of sea captains all of whom were great whalers back in the day; and how he was the nonconformist for turning to politics instead. To look at Mr Harrold he did have a pirate look about him, with his large frame and even larger beard.

With dinner finished the gentlemen retired into a separate room towards the back of the house, whilst Mrs Harrold, or Margaret as she insisted on being called, guided the ladies into a small sitting room located to the front of the house. I sat myself down in the window seat, and soon my hand was cradling yet another glass of wine. Not being familiar with any of the ladies, I was instantly the target for many questions. How did Albert and I meet? When did we get married? Do we have children? I soon realised that despite being over two hundred miles away from home, the conversations between the women at these kinds of gatherings are all the same. Thankfully I managed to give such vague answers that they ultimately lost interest in me. Being friends they all broke off into various conversations in which I couldn't make much contribution.

It was getting late and Albert had still not come to collect me. I was getting tired and wanted to leave. I knew he would be in the other room with all the men, smoking, drinking and no doubt gambling. I stared out the window; the darkness was all that could be seen, as well as my refection off the glass.

'Would you like a top up my dear?' My attention from the window was disturbed by Margaret, she held in her hand a freshly opened bottle of wine, and before I could reject her offer she had already refilled my glass. I watched her walk away from me offering more wine to her other guests, and for a split second I was in my own little world, wishing amongst anything else that I was somewhere else, ideally my bed.

I slowly turned back to the window, happy to continue in my own little world when my eyes met *His*. Only centimetres away from my own face on the opposite side of the glass, glaring back in at me... was the man from the pier. I screamed and jumped back in horror, dropping my glass on the floor; I stumbled back away from the window and tripped over the hem of my dress, before falling and banging my head against a small coffee table filled with empty wine glasses and landing in a heap on the floor.

D.

# CHAPTER 20

After the close encounter at the ruins I decided to keep my distance for the remainder of the day. I needed to think of a way to see her again, with her husband out of the way.

I made my way to the west cliff side of town where I intended to spend the rest of the day. It was very rare I came to this side of the town.

The wind was picking up as afternoon turned into evening and clouds of sand blew from the beach below, causing my eyes to water and sting in pain. The cold winter chill coming from the North Sea was bitter and had people fleeing for the warmth of their homes.

I watched in the dimming light as the wild tide crashed against the coastline, and I soon found myself seated in the dark looking out towards the sea that was no longer visible through vast darkness, yet the sound of the waves could still be heard.

The night time brings with it a new kind of atmosphere that arouses me; the stillness of the night allows me the peace and quiet I crave. Consumed by my own thoughts I am safe in the knowledge that I will not be disturbed. Even the large gulls that dominate the skies and echo their ear splitting call throughout the town are now gone for the night, I am in complete silence.

Suddenly the calm was broken by the sound of horse hooves clattering against the cobbled road. I turned to see a single horse drawn carriage coming towards me, a small lamp fixed upon it guiding them through the murky streets. I instantly recognised the driver as young Tom. My heart suddenly began to race and my eyes widened in anticipation; was it her? Had she travelled over to the west cliff?

I watched as they passed me by, unaware of my presence as I lingered within the shadows. I looked on as they continued down the street, and I began to follow, keeping my distance, eager to know if my Victoria was in fact inside.

The carriage pulled up outside a grand row of houses, and immediately her husband emerged from the carriage, followed gracefully by her. I had purposely come to this side of town to avoid any temptation surrounding her, and here she was before me once again. Fate has brought her to me. He is giving me a sign that I am right, she needs to be claimed for my own, she needs to be set free from the monster she calls her husband.

I watched as they walked up to the door and headed inside. She looked as beautiful as ever.

Tom quickly pulled the horse to the end of the street and climbed inside the carriage, awaiting their return. I could not help myself but sit myself upon an opposing wall and wait. I longed to see her again, and I began to wonder if I would be able to steal her away tonight.

It was quite some time later when a light appeared in the front living room, and suddenly there she was sitting upon the window, resembling the most beautiful mannequin London had to offer. Her skin soft and smooth, her lips luscious red and her hair pinned up with a delicate clip, she gleamed in the light; how I longed to touch her. Her beauty was beyond anything I had seen before. How I have longed to find a woman as beautiful as her, not only on the outside, but on the inside. I needed to show her that I too was just as beautiful on the inside, and that we were destined to be together. Her husband could never love her as much as I do. My desire to touch her was great, but my longing to keep her was much greater.

I continued gazing at her for what seemed the longest of times, and after a while she too looked out of the window, her eyes looking longingly in my direction. I was almost certain she was smiling at me. She turned back to the room, distracted by one of the other women. Without hesitation I crossed the road and climbed the stone steps, leaning over towards the window in which she sat. I was so close to her that I could almost smell her enchanting aroma, my face just inches from her own. At that moment she turned and looked me directly in the face. She jumped and screamed, causing me to lose my balance on the window's ledge and fall backwards, landing at the bottom of the steps in a heap. I quickly got to my feet and headed back across the street where I knew I would be hidden within the darkness. I could no longer see her in the window.

## Victoria

# CHAPTER 21

I woke to find Albert knelt over me; Margaret was fanning me with a large lace fan she had been carrying with her the entire evening. The remaining ladies were all huddled around me like chickens, trying to see what was happening. I leaned into Albert's chest, my face burning up with embarrassment.

'Take me back,' I whispered to him, giving his hand a gentle squeeze, and without a moment's hesitation Albert helped me to my feet, quickly thanked Mr Harrold for his hospitality, and led me towards the door. Albert did not even stop to put on his coat as he handed me my hat, put his own scarf around my shoulder and guided me through the doorway and back into the silence of the night.

The moment we emerged back onto the street Albert let out a loud whistle, and before I knew it Tom was pulling the horses alongside the house once more. I walked down the stone steps with caution. I was still slightly dazed and the fresh cold air began to make me feel light headed. Albert refused to let go of my hand until I was back inside the carriage, and Tom held open the door for me. Despite being within the safety of the carriage I was still wary of my surrounding. *He* was out there somewhere, and I had no way of knowing just how close he was.

I could hear my heart beating so fast that I nearly missed Albert speaking to me. My breathing had become heavier as I realised the state of panic I was still in. I was shaking, and not just from the cold. The carriage had barely moved when Albert began asking questions.

'What happened back there, V?' His voice was filled with concern, his eyes piercing my own in a desperate bid to know the truth. I sat in silence. I couldn't even bring myself to look at him. My body continued to shake, and I could no longer hide the quivering of my lips as I tried hard to fight back any tears. Albert saw straight through this pretence and pulled me in once more, his large arms embraced me as I burst into tears.

Could I really tell him the truth? Or would he just think I was just overreacting? Or worse going crazy?

By the time we had arrived back at the White Horse and Griffin and I had managed to dry my tears. After a quick thank you to Tom I dashed as quickly as possible into the inn and up the creaky wooden staircase towards our room, Albert following closely behind.

I barely spoke the remainder of the night as we got ourselves ready for bed. Albert was clearly worried about me and insisted that I tell him what had happened. However I avoided the conversation at all costs and got myself tucked up in bed.

Albert held me close in silence, he eventually gave up asking me what had happened, but I could tell it was only to allow me some rest. I knew the conversation was likely to be raised again in the morning. As we lay there in the silence, my own thoughts raced around and around. My head began to hurt and I felt sick.

Suddenly a low rumbling noise stopped my thoughts dead in their tracks. It was Albert snoring.

D.

# CHAPTER 22

I watched as Victoria was escorted out of the house and back into the carriage. I emerged back onto the road and watched as the carriage pulled out of the street and out of view.

Anger overcame me and I threw off my hat, tossing it to the ground in rage. She was gone again. I sat on the roadside for a moment next to my hat, feeling defeated once more.

At that moment something on the ground caught my eye. It was a lady's glove. I carefully picked it up and held it in my hand; I could still feel the warmth from it as though her delicate hand were still within it.

She must have been holding them and dropped one in the rush to get out of the cold and into the cab. I placed the glove over my own hand, and realized her nimble little hand would fit perfectly within my palm.

I lifted the glove to my face and took in the scent of her. The aroma of her glove filled my nostrils and warmed me inside. I could picture her face perfectly in my mind, her smile so warm and inviting.

Time was beginning to run out if I was to ever free her from the wrong man. I needed to act fast before she headed home. I did not know when exactly she planned to leave Whitby. Tomorrow was St Valentine's day, the perfect day to claim her for my own.

## Victoria

# CHAPTER 23

### WEDNESDAY 14TH FEBRUARY 1900

### ST VALENTINE'S DAY

I was woken abruptly by a loud crash; it was Albert trying to surprise me with a tray of breakfast, although now its contents were spread along the floor of the bedroom. I abruptly sat up in bed, startled by the sudden outburst of noise and burst into laughter at the sight of what was supposed to be a romantic gesture. Albert's cheeks flushed with embarrassment as my laughter gradually got worse. My eyes began to water and I held my stomach through the pain of laughter. Albert eventually smirked at my hysteria and soon found himself laughing too.

With my laughter finally under control I jumped out of bed and began helping to clear up the mess. Somehow the large china teapot had gone unharmed, and very little tea had escaped the spout; the two china cups had bounced under the bed, yet surprisingly were still in one piece. However the same could not be said for the bowl of porridge; the bowl had cracked and the porridge had landed in a heap on the floor, some had even managed to splatter against the bottom of the bed covers. A plate once filled with bacon had smashed, and the bacon pieces had tumbled across the floor landing beside the small heap of ash below the fireplace. There was also a single red rose that had been sitting on the silver tray, this too had taken a harsh fall and now laid on the floor snapped in half and its petals bent.

'I'm sorry for waking you so abruptly darling,' Albert's voice was filled with genuine regret.

'Not to worry.' I said whilst pouring a cup of tea for each of us.

'Happy Valentine's Day.' He held out the snapped rose towards me, the flower bent back on itself and resting against Albert's wrist, I immediately laughed again.

We had never really celebrated Valentine's Day, so breakfast in bed with a single red rose was certainly an unexpected surprise. I had made Albert promise me on the lead up to our first Valentines not to get me anything lavish, as he very rarely needed an opportunity to buy me something, and that simple gestures were more appreciated. To this day he has kept his word and I am always grateful for allowing the day to pass.

With the bedroom finally in a clean state once more, we both settled back on top of the bed covers with our cups of tea.

'I have a gift for you.' Albert confessed, looking amused with himself.

'I thought we agreed no gifts?' Albert's face only but lit up more in the pleasure of surprising me. He leapt from the bed and headed for the wardrobe, a smile splashed across his face the entire way. He began to rummage through one of his jacket pockets, and quickly pulled out a long, thin, square box. He handed it to me quickly. He did not speak but looked at me playfully, like a schoolboy who had just received a gold star. There was a sparkle in his eyes and a hint of cheekiness in his smile.

'I hope you like it,' he said as I began to inspect the

fairly large yet thin box; it was black leather with a small clasp on top holding it closed. I released the clasp and the top of the box opened up like two small double doors, revealing the hidden surprise inside.

I gasped when I saw its content; it was the most beautiful Whitby Jet necklace I had ever seen. The delicate black oval beads shimmered within the box, and a large tear shaped pendant hung at the bottom, its deep black texture hard and strong as I lifted it from the box, yet not cold to the touch as I had expected. It caught the light beautifully giving it a silky soft appearance.

'This is too much,' I finally said. 'Albert it is beautiful.' He did not speak, but smiled warmly at me, clearly pleased with himself.

I soon began looking through my many dresses, trying to decide which would show off my new necklace the best. I finally decided on my black day dress; with its slightly lower neckline and laced edges I knew the necklace would sit perfectly against it.

'What would you care to do today?' I asked Albert as we continued to get ourselves ready. He looked up at me sheepishly from the desk he was now perched at.

'I'm sorry, V, I have been invited to attend another

meeting at lunchtime, and probably won't get back until late afternoon.' He genuinely looked rather upset as he told me this, yet I still could not hide the misery from my face.

'I will make it up to you tomorrow; it is our last full day before we head home on Friday, so we will make sure to do something fun that you want to do.'

I did not reply; I just sat on the edge of the bed avoiding his eye contact. I knew he would do something like this; how could he call this a late honeymoon when he was going off to various meetings the entire trip?

It wasn't long until Albert had left, and I was again alone in our room wondering what to do with myself. After the events of last night I found myself hesitant to leave the Inn. I had managed to brush the conversation aside and kept Albert from knowing what really happened, despite him trying to ask on numerous occasions. Who was this man that kept appearing? Our first encounter seemed relevantly normal, if you could call it that, for he walked me back to the inn when it was dark and was a perfect gentleman. Not once during that short walk did I feel threatened or intimidated by him. Maybe it was my imagination playing tricks on me; maybe I was over thinking the whole thing.

I decided I would take my library book and find a nice quiet spot to read outside, at the same time getting some much needed fresh air. Despite the bedroom being nice, it did feel a little cramped and stuffy after a while. I was certainly in the need of some air.

Upon leaving the inn I ran straight into young Tom who was on his way inside to see Mr Walker.

'Beg yer pardon, Miss,' he said 'I hope I didn't startle ya.'

I smiled warmly at him.

'Good morning Tom, how are you today?'

'Very well thank ya Mrs Summers, headed anywhere in particular Miss?' he asked with genuine interest.

'I thought I would take a walk and find a quiet spot to read my book.'

'May I recommend a place?' His eyes lit up as though excited to tell me.

'Of course,' I replied, eager to know where he would send me.

'If tha continues along Church Street, tha come's to a small street just past'd 199 steps. It leads down towards East pier, but before you go down to the pier there's a bench that overlooks the harbour entrance. It's rare folk go that way as there are no shops, but the view of the piers is one of the best,' he explained.

'Thank you Tom, I may have to investigate this bench, sounds like just the spot I'm looking for.' And with that he wished me a pleasant day and hurried on inside.

Church Street was again busy, full of people of all ages going about their everyday lives. The atmosphere in town this morning was cheerful, and, as ever, many people I did not know wished me a good morning as I passed them. Whitby was indeed the friendliest place I had ever visited.

As I continued down Church Street I did begin to feel a little overdressed, most people in the street were working, and the ladies I passed all wore pinafores. I was the only lady dressed up smartly. I gathered that I stood out quite a bit.

I briskly continued up the street where I eventually made it to the bottom of the 199 steps. I stopped to admire them, so steep, yet so magnificent looking as they ascended up the cliff side as though they had always been there. Heading around to the left of the stairs was the small street Tom had mentioned; it was even narrower and quieter than Church Street – in fact I was the only person walking the little cobbled road. The houses that lined this street were also smaller: tiny cottages with even smaller front doors all lined the street, no front gardens only the smallest of pavements between them and the narrow road. On the first house was a plaque that named the road, Henrietta Street. I found myself rather amused by the tiny doorways. Albert would have had to bend down to get inside, and even I would have struggled not to bang my head against the top.

Finally I emerged at the end of the street, and I had a perfect view of the harbour entrance leading out to open sea. As promised a small bench was situated in the perfect position to watch the boats pass by below. The road was indeed a dead end; the pavement continued down towards the pier, but it was quite a steep slope down, and I was higher than expected, so I decided against going any further.

Taking a seat I admired the view before me and took a deep breath of air, the taste of salt lingering in my mouth, yet it did not bother me. In fact I would go as far as to say that I liked it; it was a lot more welcome than the clammy London air I was so used to.

The book I had been carrying soon drew my attention, and before long I was whisked away into the make-believe world of *The Rise of Silas Lapham* by William Dean Howells, occasionally looking up and admiring the view again.

Suddenly I was engulfed by a shadow; I was unsure how this was even possible as it was such a cloudy day to begin with. I looked up from my book, but before I knew it a hand appeared in front of my face and quickly covered my mouth, the leather glove warm against my face.

'Do not scream,' the husky voice whispered against my ear. I could feel his breath against my neck. Scared as I was I nodded in acknowledgment of his command. He moved around the bench, still holding onto me, and that is when I saw his face. His dark eyes penetrating my own again looked grey against his pale skin; a tired looking top hat hid the mess of hair poking from the sides, and the suit that he wore looked as though he had been wearing it for weeks on end.

'We need to have a serious little talk, you and I.' He spoke softly to me, yet his voice was deep and threatening. 'But not here; if you promise me not to scream I will let you go.' With my eyes bulging wide I again nodded in agreement. He removed his hand slowly, and as promised I refrained from making a sound, yet inside I was crying. My hands began to shake and my throat dried as I tried to speak.

'What do you want with me?' I finally broke my silence.

'Not here,' he said, and taking me by the hand he began to lead me away.

At that moment something inside me burst and I began to shriek. Tears fell down my face and I could no longer stop myself from making a sound. He turned to look at me, angered by my sudden outburst. He raised a threatening hand to me, but this only made my shrieking worse, and I let out a small scream.

Suddenly his hand came crashing down towards my face and he hit me across the cheek with the back of his gloved hand. I landed with a thud on the cobbled road, banging my head against the hard surface; and when I awoke, I was no longer in the middle of the street.

D.

# CHAPTER 24

I couldn't believe my eyes when I saw Her sitting on a bench reading. What had brought her to this corner of the town? There was nothing here. As my eyes focused upon her I knew this was possibly my best opportunity. It was the perfect time to claim her for my own.

Maybe this is why she had come, in hope that I would find her and we could be alone.

I crept up behind her and stood there for a moment in silence, watching her as she glanced between her book and the sea view before her. I was hesitant as to how to break the silence, unsure how to start a conversation with her, I couldn't charge in and declare my love to her straight away. She had not realised I was standing behind her, so to avoid any unnecessary screaming I decided it was best to hold her mouth until she had got used to my being there. She was certainly shocked by my sudden arrival, but I promised to let her go if she did not scream.

'What do you want with me?' she asked.

'Not here,' I replied. I didn't like the idea of talking about us in broad daylight. It is not wise for a married woman to be seen talking to another man without the presence of her husband; I knew we were best speaking somewhere more private.

I took her by her hand, a small dainty hand that fit perfectly within my own, and began to lead her away. We did not get far however before she began having a panic attack. Her breathing became more rapid and her entire body became rigid as though her feet were stuck to the ground. I had heard about these before, but had never witnessed somebody having one. I was certain that the trick was to shock them out of it. I did not want to hit her, so I threatened to slap her first in hope that would calm her. However this seemed to make things worse and she began to scream. Hesitant of wanting to harm her, I took a deep breath and slapped her hard across the face. My heart sank the moment my hand impacted upon her face. She stumbled backwards and landed hard on the ground, her head slamming against the cobbled bricks and knocking her unconscious.

'No!' I hollered, and threw myself upon her. 'I am sorry my love, please forgive me.' I threw my arms around her and pulled her motionless body into me. I could still hear her breathing gently, and her heart was racing hard when I placed my hand against her chest. It was then I noticed the necklace around her beautiful neck, instantly recognisable as Whitby Jet; a gift from her husband no doubt.

I lifted her chin and looked at her. She was so radiant. She could have almost been mistaken for sleeping within my arms she looked so peaceful. I kissed her gently upon the forehead before trying to move her. I knew it was not safe to keep her on the ground; she needed to be somewhere safe. I took her into my arms before carrying her away. She will be safe with me; I will make sure of that.

Tom

# CHAPTER 25

I was headed into the inn to speak with Mr Walker, and in the doorway bumped into Mrs Summers. She was always so cheerful and seemed pleased to speak to me for a moment.

'Good morning Tom, how are you today?' Her voice was very posh, and her clothes always looked perfect.

'Very well thank ya Mrs Summers, you going anywhere nice?' I asked her, it was rare she went anywhere without Mr Summers.

'I thought I would take a walk and find a quiet spot to read my book' was her reply; I quickly suggested a bench which overlooked the piers, to which she seemed pleased, before wishing me a good day and departing.

I entered the inn. Mr Walker was in his office as he often was, I knocked on the door and a soft 'come in' could be heard coming from the other side.

'Mr Walker I have just come to…'

'Ahh Tom,' he interrupted me. 'I am pleased you popped in as I have a few errands for you once you've finished your duties, if you don't mind.' He wasn't really asking, more telling, but Mr Walker was always perfectly polite with me.

'That's what I was comin' to tell ya Mr Walker. I've just finished.'

'Perfect,' he said, shuffling a stack of papers littering his desk. 'Martha, the barmaid is unwell today so I am unable to leave. Could you possibly take this money down to Mrs Taylor at the corner shop, I told her I would pay her today. Also I need this telegram sending off, I will give you some money for that too. Finally a letter has arrived for Mrs Summers; would you run upstairs and hand it to her for me.'

'Mrs Summers left a couple of minutes ago, Sir, I saw her headed down the street.'

Mr Walker looked confused by this, but did not question me.

'If you like Sir I could try to catch her. She couldn't have gotten very far, and I think I know where she was headed.'

Mr Walker smiled at me and handed over the items. He didn't speak again but waved his hand gesturing for me to leave his office. I dashed out of the inn at full speed and raced up the street in the direction I knew she had taken.

By the time I had reached Henrietta Street I was exhausted and my running turned into a slow walk. My heart was pounding from my chest and my mouth dry. As I neared the end of the street I could hear voices. One was instantly recognisable as Mrs Summers' but I could not make out the other.

I pressed myself against the row of houses and peered around the corner to see who was there. My eyes quickly fixed upon two people standing beside the bench: Mrs Summers and a man who I did not know, but was not her husband. Mrs Summers was clearly distressed as she let out a small panicked scream. I hesitated, and suddenly the man's hand came crashing down, hitting her hard across the face. She fell to the ground with a crash and immediately I retreated back behind the house out of sight. I tried to hear what was going on, but the man's voice was low and I could not make out his words.

I slowly began backing up the road, I did not want him to hear my footsteps but I knew I needed to get help fast, before it was too late.

Detective Matthews

# CHAPTER 26

After the events of Monday, I had spent a considerable amount of my Tuesday questioning people who knew the young girl who had been found in the ally. I had also returned to speak to the fishmonger who had found her body. Yet despite all these extra efforts I was still no further into finding anything.

By lunchtime, myself and Constable Taylor, who had been taking down notes, found ourselves wandering the streets. I could barely focus on Taylor's voice as he relayed to me his scribbled handwriting. My mind was still racing round and round with the hurtful insults the parents of the murdered girl had thrown at me. I started to feel personally responsible for her murder. It has been over six weeks since the first girl was found dead and here I was walking the cobbled streets still none the wiser as to who was responsible.

'Detective Matthews!' a small voice called out from behind me, stopping my thoughts dead and bringing me back to the present. It was a young boy running up the street towards me, waving with all his might to ensure he caught my attention.

'Detective Matthews, wait!' he shouted again, as he approached me breathless. I was certain I recognised him and it took me a couple of seconds to place him as the young lad who worked at the White Horse and Griffin.

'Can I help you young man?'

He tried to speak while catching his breath. 'It's Mrs Summers... the lady from London who's stayin' at the inn... Sir.'

'What about her, boy?'

'I think she is in trouble, I think she needs your help!' he shouted with rage and fear in his voice.

'Speak clearly boy. What exactly did you see?'

'A man, talkin' to her. He was angry and hit her.' I

had heard more than enough.

'Lead the way, now.'

He grabbed me by the arm and led me back the way he had come, turning me onto Church Street we sprinted along the road at full speed.

'Can you describe what you saw?' I asked the young boy, and at that point I suddenly remembered his name. 'Tom, isn't it?' I queried. 'Talk me through what you saw Tom?' Constable Taylor sprinted to keep up, his notepad raised as he scribbled away frantically.

'She was talking to a strange man...she seemed upset...he hit her.' His words were only just understandable as he tried to talk and run at the same time, his breathing gradually thickening and becoming more prominent. He guided us along Henrietta Street in the direction of the East Pier. At the end of the street Tom ground to a sudden stop, and we were faced with nothing but a bench, and a view out towards the piers.

'Well?' I said, waiting for him to say something.

'They were right here.' He spoke with worry in his voice, his eyes searching down towards the deserted pier in the hope of seeing her. My own mind froze, if Tom was indeed telling the truth then where could they have gone, and worse what was he going to do to her.

'Let us head back to the inn Tom. I need to speak to Mr Summers, and we need to find Mrs Summers as soon as possible. Is there anything else you can remember, what was said, or perhaps what this man looked like?' I held the young boy by the shoulders and lowered my face so it was adjacent to his. Tom's face looked lost as he tried to think hard.

'He spoke so quiet. I heard Mrs Summers scream, and then he hit her. I remember seeing him in a top hat and coat, but nothing more I can recall.' Tears began to form in Tom's eyes, he was clearly upset that he had not been able to help further.

'Listen to me Tom, I need you to go back to the inn and stay safe; myself and Constable Taylor will take things from here. However I do not want to cause panic within the town, so you need to promise me, Tom, that you will go straight back without telling anybody about this, alright?' I could not believe I was asking a child to keep such a promise; his eyes looked as though they could cry at any moment as he nodded silently in response to my question.

We briskly walked back along Henrietta Street, Tom did not speak the entire way, and as we reached the White Horse and Griffin he paused, clearly unsure what to do with himself.

'I need to speak to Mr Summers, Tom; you are more than welcome to run along if you wish.' I did not want him to feel he had to stay; he had already been through enough already.

'I want to help find Mrs Summers,' he said, his voice slightly more normal than before, though an air of nervousness was still apparent. 'I will take a walk and let you know if I see anything.' With that he left, walking back along the street in a brisk manner. I couldn't help but smile at his determination to help, people much older would have been happy to be left out of something like this.

I turned and entered the inn, immediately greeted by the landlord.

'Good afternoon Detective, and what can I do for you?' He barely ever smiled.

'I was hoping to speak to Mr Summers; do you happen to know where he is?' Mr Walker lifted a hand in gesture that I should wait before he turned back into his office, returning moments later with a piece of torn paper.

'Mr Summers is in a meeting at this address, he

gave me this as Tom will be picking him up later this evening.' I looked at the address in my hand; I knew exactly where it was and flew out of the door clutching the paper tightly, thanking Mr Walker as I dashed out the door. Constable Taylor had stayed behind at the inn.

Nearly ten minutes later I finally reached the address on the West side of town, and I was exhausted after running the entire way.

I banged on the door repeatedly until it was finally opened by an elderly woman, her face startled at the sight of me gasping for air on the door step.

'I am Detective Matthews. I am looking for Mr Albert Summers. Do you know if he is here?' The woman did not speak but bowed her head in acknowledgment before turning back into the hallway, leaving the door slightly ajar. I stood waiting on the doorstep, anxious that they were to hurry. Finally Mr Summers appeared at the door.

'Is everything alright here Detective?' His voice filled with a mild anger as though unimpressed at my interruption of his meeting.

'Mr Summers, I need you to come with me. It

concerns your wife.'

'Victoria?' His eyes widened and his face fell at the sheer thought of there being something wrong.

'What's happened?' he demanded.

'Please Mr Summers, if you would come with me, I will explain everything I know on the way.'

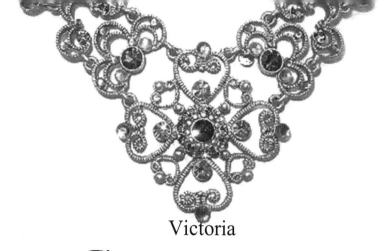

## Victoria

# CHAPTER 27

**I** woke to the smell of burning, but not the kind attached to a fire, more of an incense being burnt to cause an aroma. My head was pounding and my eyes took a long time to adjust to the dim light of the single candle that lit the room I was in. Next to it was the burning stick that was scenting the room, the smoke of which danced around the candle flame in a blue smoke before rising higher and disappearing up into the darkness.

I looked down at myself to find I was laid in what looked like a bed, yet it was so narrow and short I barely fit. I was covered in what felt like silk bed sheets, soft and smooth to the touch as though never been used. As I admired the sheets I realised that the attractive aroma filling the room was lavender. Floral and sweet with a strange relaxing feel to it. I still had on my long dress and shoes, despite almost being tucked in.

I strained my eyes around the gloomy room, trying my hardest to make out anything else. A single chair was positioned next to the small round table upon which the candle sat. I scanned the room but could not see any further beyond the candle as the room continued into darkness; I looked for a door that would let me escape.

I launched myself to get out of the bed, intending to pick up the candle in the aim to use it to guide me. Walking from the bed, I had overestimated how far away the candle was, and was starting to realise just how vast the room was. As I approached the table I was overcome with the smoky scents coming from the burning stick and began to cough violently. I went to grab the metal candle holder, but it was stuck hard to the table. I tried to force it but the holder did not move, and the table it sat upon also did not budge under my efforts. Why would anybody stick a candle to the table? And what's worse, why would they stick the table to the floor?

I began to scan the room once more, still hoping that a way out would become apparent. Nothing. How had I got here?

The darkness circled the small table and it was difficult to make out how far away the dark walls actually were. I began to walk past the table, away from the bed and the light, holding out my hands in the darkness so as not to walk into the wall. The room was without doubt much bigger than I had initially thought, and by the time I had reached a wall I could no longer see the bed hidden in the darkness, now at the opposite side of the room. The walls were damp, cold and rough, like one would expect to see inside a cave. A sudden draught caught hold of me causing me to shiver. I could barely see my own hands in front of me.

Desperate to leave, I began feeling my way along the harsh walls, in hopes that an opening I had missed would appear. As I ran my hands over the cold surface I could sense my fingers becoming more numb and tender with every movement. The walls were ice cold, and as I moved along the dampness worsened, leaving my entire hands soaked. Suddenly my fingers brushed against something soft, warm even. It was a fabric, almost like a giant dark curtain camouflaged against the rock like walls. I ran my hand over it many times, taking pleasure from the warm softness against my now throbbing fingers, yet I was hesitant to pull it aside through fear of what may lie beyond.

Eventually my fingers found the edge of the fabric and I pulled it to one side. It was heavy and I needed to use all my strength to move it. I was faced with a small passage, so small it was barely a couple of feet long, and at the end another dark fabric drape, only this time I could see light squeezing its way around the edges. I took hold of the screen and with both hands I again moved it to one side with all my strength. Never have I seen such heavy fabric. As the drape gave way I was hit by a ray of light, and as I edged myself through the gap I found myself in a large open room. The centre of the floor was filled with more than ten solid silver candelabras, all of which were taller than me, and each with six perfectly white long thin melting candles lit upon them. The flames danced in unison as the draught followed me through the curtained passage.

My eyes were wide in astonishment as I took in the room before me: the ceiling was so high that it could not be seen as it rose into a vast never ending darkness. The walls, similar to the other room, were cold damp exposed stone. They were decorated in streaks of green moss and algae climbing up towards the darkness. The uneven floor was littered with newspaper clippings old and new, and one of the walls had various clippings stuck to it too. I cautiously moved myself closer to this wall, and it became instantly apparent that the entire wall of newspaper clippings related to the same thing: the murders happening in Whitby. I looked closer at the clippings and started reading them. All of the victims had been women in their twenties. Each article relayed a similar story, the only difference being that of the victim's name; and all articles pleading for anybody to come forward with information. It suddenly dawned on me exactly who this man must be.

As I came to the end of the display I gasped with shock at what I saw: it was a hand drawn picture, of me.

'I see you have found your portrait.' His voice startled me as it echoed against the dull walls. I felt a gentle hand placed on my shoulder. I jumped back from his grip and turned to look at him.

'What do you want with me?' I demanded.

'My dear, you were hurt, I needed to get you somewhere safe.'

'And you think kidnapping me was the best thing to do?' My voice was shaking, yet I could not contain the anger that was burning up inside me. He looked at me as though I had hurt his feelings, as though I was the one to overstep the mark. He turned his back and began walking away.

'Wait!' I shouted, he stopped in his tracks but did not turn to face me. 'What are you going to do with me?'

'Me?' He turned and questioned me as though I was talking nonsense. 'I am not going to do anything. It is you that must correct the mistakes you have made and set right the path in which you deserve to live.' I looked at him puzzled. What was he talking about? He walked back towards me and grabbed my hand faster than I could pull it away.

'I know your feelings must be difficult to hide from me.' He began caressing my hand against his face as he spoke to me. 'But I do not blame you for the mistakes you have made. I am here now to set you free and let you live the life you truly deserve.'

I pulled my hand back, but his grip was too strong.

He leaned into me, pressing me against the wall of paper clippings, his hand stroking my hair.

'You are far too beautiful to be wasted on a man like him. I have seen the way you look at me but I cannot be responsible for your own infidelity. You must leave him, so that we can be together.' He leaned into me and gently touched his lips against my neck, inhaling loudly and taking in my scent. I pushed him back, but this only caused him to laugh in my face.

He finally let me go and snatched the picture he had drawn of me off the wall.

'I had always enjoyed drawing, but I have not found the inspiration for it in such a long time.' He turned back to me and looked me straight in the eye. 'You have reawakened this love in me, and I will draw you again and again.'

'What is your name?' I have no idea why this was my next question, but I thought by keeping him talking that I might distract him from touching me again. He took a step back from me and made a disgusted sound as though I had said something offensive.

'A name is but a label bestowed on you by the ghastly people that bear you into this world, a label that they forced on you, and one that you must live with for the rest of your Godforsaken life. No thought or regards as to whether you would like it. Well not me. I have no name. I refuse to be known by the name those bastards cursed me with.' His voice was getting louder and louder as it echoed off the walls, his anger was mounting and I could tell that he was about to lash out at any minute. I needed to stop him.

'So what do I call you?' I uttered, almost wanting to kick myself the moment it came out of my mouth. Fearful that this would upset him further.

He paused for a moment as though shocked by my question. 'D,' was his only reply, as he walked away from me. Removing the hat from his head he placed it down on a large wooden desk I had not noticed. His hair was curly and dark brown, and was long enough to just sit over his ears.

His face was youthful, yet it looked tired and worn as though he had suffered a hard life, his eyes dark and tiresome yet his gaze was hard and demanding; never had I seen a man with grey eyes such as his. As I looked up on this seemingly lonely man I found myself feeling sorry for him. He was clearly unwell, and looking at the tiredness of his clothing he did not have much money. Yet to look at him he seemed perfectly normal. In fact I would almost go as far as to say he was handsome. He was tall and broad chested, yet strangely slender due to his height. How had this man turned into such a recluse, and into the man the Whitby residents thought him?

'You know what you must do?' He looked at me from the desk. I had not moved from the clippings pinned to the wall, and was unsure whether to or not.

'I'm sorry,' I said, uncertain of what he was asking of me.

'You are to speak to your husband and tell him you are leaving him. I will be waiting for you so we can be together.' His voice was serious, yet I desperately wanted to question his sincerity. How were we to be together, he was a monster, a murderer? I could not be with him even if I wanted to be.

I paused and looked at him in horror. He did not speak again but simply waited for my reply. I knew that if I was to escape I needed to play along. He was offering me the chance to go speak to Albert, and that was enough for me.

'Yes.' I said cautiously, I was a bad liar and hoped he would not see through my plan to leave. 'I will go and speak to Albert.'

His eyes lit up at my words. He rushed towards me and took me in his arms, lifting me off the ground and spinning me around before pulling my face into his own and kissing me hard on the lips.

'But sir, we cannot be together until I have spoken to my husband. Restrain yourself.' I hated having to lie, but I needed to at least look as though I was interested in him, even if it was just to get myself out.

'It is late now. You slept for a long time, and you must go,' he said to me as he stuck the picture of me back on the wall. 'We do not want them to worry about you.' And he took my hand and led me over to his desk. He paused a second before opening the top drawer, then pulled out my library book, handing it to me. In the split second he held out my book, I could almost see the normal man inside him; his face softened, his brow relaxed and for the first time he seemed happy. What was I going to do?

'Now you must go, and tell him you are leaving.' He held me by the shoulders and spoke to me in whispers as though not wanting to be heard by anyone but me; he then pulled me in again and kissed me on the mouth. His lips were strangely warm as he held my face to his own, yet I pulled my face away.

He said something else as he reached back into the drawer of his desk, but I did not quite catch the words he spoke. Suddenly he brought out a small cutting of fabric and quickly pushed it onto my face, holding it against my mouth and nose whilst his other hand held me firmly in place. I struggled to escape his grip, but he was too strong for me. The overwhelming scent of the cloth caused me to feel faint, before I finally blacked out.

D.

# Chapter 28

I watched from the shadows as she entered the candle-lit room, her eyes squinting as they adjusted to the sudden light intensity of the room. Her attention was quickly taken by the wall of newspaper clippings I had so carefully arranged. Her graceful movements were a pleasure to watch as she made her way to take a closer look. She had not even noticed me in the corner, concealed by the shadow of the curved wall. I watched her for a moment as she took in the clippings, reading them casually as though she had all the time in the world. As I made my way over to her I caught her eyes move over the portrait I have drawn of her. Such a shame I had not thought to hide it, I could have given it to her as a gift.

'I see you have found your portrait,' I said, and she jumped; clearly unaware I had been standing behind her.

'What do you want with me?' she demanded, anger clear in her voice.

'My dear, you were hurt, I needed to get you somewhere safe,' I replied trying to calm her.

'And you think kidnapping me was the best thing to do?'

I was shocked by her response. I did not kidnap her; I was merely trying to keep her safe. I could never have left her on the ground unconscious. What kind of man would that make me, to leave a loved one behind in such time of need? I turned and walked away, hurt, unsure how to proceed in our conversation.

'Wait!' she called after me. 'What are you going to do with me?'

'Me?' I stumbled at her question, confused by it almost. 'I am not going to do anything. It is you that must correct the mistakes you have made and set right the path in which you deserve to live.' She somehow seemed to relax more as our conversation continued, and I leaned in and kissed her gently on the neck, her aroma filling my nostrils, my desire for her growing ever more.

I explained that she must tell her husband the truth, we both knew her true feelings for me and I could not see her disgrace her own name just because she was in an unhappy marriage. She needed to tell him the truth so she could be with me fully.

I was surprised at her enthusiasm towards telling him. Her eyes danced with sheer happiness when I told her we would be together at last once he knew. I took her by the hand and led her over to my desk. Her library book was in my top drawer for safe keeping, and I handed it back to her. I knew I had to figure a way of getting her out of here without her knowing where the entrance was; after all if her fool of a husband was to trick her and follow her back then we would both be in trouble.

I suddenly recalled having a rag in my desk, drenched in high fragranced toxin that would knock anybody unconscious. I had used it numerous time and knew this was the only way, although I hated the thought of doing it to her. I saw it needed to be done fast, and so I leaned back and grabbed the rag as quickly as I could, pushing it into her face and holding her steady so she could not escape. As predicted she was unconscious in seconds. I held her tight so as not to let her fall. Her library book which had fallen to the ground I held onto with my free hand, and I proceeded to carry her back outside.

As I carried her I could not stop looking upon her beautiful face. I knew it was only a matter of time before she would admit to her true feelings; and it now won't be long until she belongs to me.

Victoria

# CHAPTER 29

**M**y eyes were heavy and sore as I woke, my entire body stiff and uncomfortable. As my eyes finally adjusted to my surroundings I realised I was back on the bench overlooking the two piers, and the moody looking ocean beyond. My library book had been placed onto the seat next to me.

I looked around to see if anybody was around, but the immediate area was deserted. Silence was instantly noticeable, even the scream of the seagulls could not be heard echoing from the harbour like normal. I slowly stood from the old wooden bench, my back sore as though I had been sitting there for hours and my legs slightly shaky. It was now dark out, and any hope of light had been absorbed by the darkened clouds hanging motionless in the sky. I snatched my book from the bench and briskly began to walk back in the direction of town. I stumbled as I began to walk, a slight wobble in my exhausted legs as if suffering from a long night of wine drinking. I stopped and held onto the bench whilst I recomposed myself, my head spinning and my vision slightly blurred. Nausea fell upon me. I set off again but had to stop again quite soon to prevent myself from tumbling to the ground; I leaned against the first little house to avoid falling over.

Suddenly as I stood leant against the wall, memories of *Him* flooded back to me. His hands were touching me, his face so close to my own breathing in my scent, and his lips caressing my neck and kissing my lips as though he had the right to them. Goosebumps suddenly spread across my entire body as I remember his irrational request for me to run away with him. How could he be so blind to think that I would want to elope with somebody like him, his delusion baffled me.

I finally caught my balance and began to slowly run down the narrow street and in the direction of the inn; my adrenaline was high as I raced along the cobbles, and in no time I was passing the base of the 199 steps. I turned onto Church Street without a single hesitation. I continued at an almighty speed along the dark road, holding up my dress to ensure I didn't trip over it. The street was now empty of other people, my heels and heavy gasping the only noise to be heard.

I arrived outside the White Horse and Griffin and without a moment to spare I burst through the door and ran straight into a gentleman on his way out of the inn. He caught me in his arms and managed to stop us both from tumbling to the ground. My book fell onto the floor and fell open to a random page, and a small card fell from it, landing onto the floor next to it.

'I'm sorry sir.' I hesitated, embarrassed by my charging into him; however his eyes were no longer on me, but the card which had fallen out of my book.

'Madam, may I ask where you acquired this card?' His deep voice was stern and of a serious nature. I looked to the ground and stared at the card lying limp on the stone floor. No bigger than a playing card it depicted a small pencil drawing of a large black dog. The gentleman knelt to pick up the card from the ground, clearly keen to inspect it further. He turned it over to reveal a large 'D' in a strange red substance; surely it wasn't blood?

The gentleman turned his attention back to me, and spoke with a more urgent tone to his voice. 'Where did you get this card?' I opened my mouth to reply to his question, but I could not find my voice, at that moment Albert entered the room. 'V, where on earth have you been, I've been worried sick about you.' He took hold of my hands and pulled me into his broad chest, holding me tighter than he had ever done before. I could not hold my emotions in a moment longer and immediately burst into tears.

When I had finally composed myself, Albert sat me down in the bar area and asked Mr Walker to bring me a warm drink, my hands were trembling and had begun turning blue from the utter cold.

'Darling this is Detective Matthews, we have spent the entire afternoon looking for you.' Matthews greeted me with a slight nod of the head and slightly moving the corner of the hat which sat proudly upon his head. A younger man entered the inn and without hesitation pulled up a chair to join us.

'Ah yes, Mrs Summers, this is Constable Taylor,'

the detective said, 'he has been working closely with me in the search for you today.' I give the Constable a friendly smile to acknowledge his introduction.

'Pleased to meet you madam,' he stretched out his hand to shake my own; 'and may I say how pleased I am to see you back safe.' His voice had less authority to it than the detectives, and his round boyish face did not seem to fit against the smart suit he wore. Detective Matthews sat forward in his chair, his arms rested on the small round table that swayed somewhat due to its uneven legs, and he cleared his throat as though ready to make a long speech.

'Mrs Summers I was wondering if you would be willing to answer a couple of questions?' Matthews spoke with such confidence and reassurance about him that it was difficult for me to decline.

'What is it you wish to know?'

The Detective slid the small card into the centre of the table, the bright red 'D' staring up at me.

'Do you know what this is?' he asked. His stern voice and hard stare made me feel like I was the one in trouble.

'I have never seen it before.' It was the truth, yet somehow as it left my mouth it sounded very much like a lie. Albert took my hand and sandwiched it between his own.

'Darling, you need to tell us everything that happened to you today, it's serious.'

'Mrs Summers maybe it would be better if I told you what I already know about this card, and why I am so keen to discover where you got it from.'

I nodded weakly, for it was getting very late and I was more exhausted than I had realised.

'On December 28th a young lady, aged only 17 years old, was found dead in a small alley not too far from here. Over the following six weeks many other women have been murdered, all in a similar way. Our only clue that links one person to all of these murders is cards identical to this one. The murderer has left one behind with his victim's body each time.'

Matthews held up the card and made a point of shaking it with anger before slamming it back onto the table with a loud thud. His frustration on the subject apparent, and his own exhaustion clear, the dark circles under his eyes told me that he had not slept well in several weeks.

'As it stands we cannot find any connection between these women or a reason why they had been targeted. No prior warnings, threats or indications had been made to them nor any indication given where the next target was going to be attacked. At the beginning of this week another victim was found only a short walk from here.'

Matthews paused, he stared at the card in which he still held onto firmly. 'Mrs Summers, I understand that the man responsible for all this may not have handed you this card directly, but I am concerned that he did slip it into your book. If this is the case then I fear that you may have become a target.'

I nearly burst into laughter. I wasn't even sure why, nothing that had been said was funny, not even in the slightest. Yet I had an almighty urge to fall into a sudden array of hysterical laughter. I decided it was the exhaustion playing tricks with me, hoping that what I was being told was some kind of practical joke and the events of the last twenty-four hours had all been one big hoax.

Matthews did not speak again, his face stern, waiting for my reply. I sat in silence for a moment, unsure what exactly to say.

'I do not know who this man is' was how I broke the silence. I could not look at Albert as I started to relive the story, firstly telling Detective Matthews of my meeting this man earlier in the week as he walked with me from the lighthouse, and how he had escorted me all the way back to the inn. 'He was a perfect gentleman and did not do anything to cause me any reason to panic that night,' I told Matthews. All the while Constable Taylor frantically wrote in his note book, the scratching sound of his pencil against the paper seemed loud in my ear.

I then told the detective how I was certain I had seen the man staring in the window at me during the dinner party. I then relived the encounter with him today, how he had crept up on me whilst reading my book and kidnapped me, releasing me only on the promise that I would leave Albert and elope with him; promising him I would, knowing it was my only chance of escape. I also tried to describe his appearance only to be blank minded as I recalled his clothing more than his actual features.

As I got to the end of my story I burst into tears once more. Albert pulled me in closer to him and tried to calm me with his soothing voice.

'You are safe now my darling, you are with me.'

'Thank you Mrs Summers for that statement. It

was a shame you did not see where this hide was, but nonetheless, this is the most information we have on him yet.' Detective Matthews certainly had a way with words, the confidence in his voice certainly made you feel as though you could trust him, but I could tell even through my tears that he had yet to formulate a plan.

'I think my wife has had enough questions for one night Detective. If you don't mind I would like her to get some rest.' Albert stood and took my hand, leading me towards the back of the bar, in the direction of the stairs.

'Very well,' Matthews responded. 'However is it possible I could have a quick talk to you before I leave? There is something I wish to get your opinion on.' Albert nodded and told Matthews he would be back down once he had seen me into bed.

Detective Matthews

# CHAPTER 30

**W**hen Albert returned he was clearly upset. His mood had changed dramatically from the concerned husband to blatant anger, and I knew it was only a matter of time before this anger unleashed itself upon me. He silently took his seat across the small table from me and looked me straight in the eye as he spoke.

'What are you planning to do about this situation Detective?' were his first words. His lips pursed together and his eyes burning with anger as he waited for me to give him answers.

'Mr Summers…I…' I paused. For some reason I

just could not find the words to say. I thought that having more information about this man would bring a tidal wave of ideas to me; I expected to know exactly what we should do next. But for some reason I was left blank. I genuinely did not know which direction was the best one to take; one wrong move and Mrs Summers could end up dead, and worse still the murderer not captured. Eventually after an awkward few seconds I cleared my throat and re-found my voice.

'I am very sorry about what has happened to your wife today, and may I say that I am extremely pleased she has been returned to you unharmed.'

Albert looked at me through narrowed eyes as though he wanted me to get to the point.

'This 'D' character has never, to our knowledge, kidnapped anybody and then released them, so I am unsure what exactly he is planning. However these attacks, as you are fully aware of have been going on now for over six weeks and I am under enormous pressure to stop the culprit before another murder is committed.'

'Please get to the point Detective, some of us want to go to bed.' Albert turned his head to look up at the large clock positioned above the bar; it read ten minutes to midnight. At that moment a plan suddenly crept into my mind, but I knew that if I had any chance in convincing him it was the right thing to do, I needed to proceed with caution.

'What we know is that Mrs Summers has been released with orders to formally leave you and run away with him, although sadly Mrs Summers does not recall he suggested a meeting place and time. I believe that if she was to return to the bench overlooking the East pier, he would not be too far away. As you may or may not know that bench is located on a dead end road, the only way to go is down to the pier, which again is a dead end, or return back up along the street.'

Albert's fist suddenly slammed down onto the table knocking over the now empty glasses, his face even more serious as he rose to his feet.

'Are you suggesting that we offer my wife up as an enticement so you can catch this mad man that has gotten away from you every time?' His voice echoed throughout the uninhabited bar, deep and fuelled with rage. He pushed his chair back and began to walk away, and I quickly grasped his arm. He turned abruptly and looked me dead into the eye, his face filled with pure anger.

'I know this is not the perfect solution Mr Summers, but unless we can lure this man out into the open where we can see him, then I am afraid that he will just go on killing.'

Albert's face softened slightly as he pulled his arm from my grip. He stood motionless for a moment, silent and eyes fixed upon the floor before returning his gaze to me, I expected him to speak but he just looked at me in silence for a minute.

'Mr Summers I beg your forgiveness for my blurting out this idea so abruptly. But as I mentioned "D" has never released a victim before, and his crazed idea that Mrs Summers will leave you and run away with him, tells me that not only is this a very sick man, but he has developed a strange infatuation with your wife where he believes she returns his feelings. I agree this is not the best of ideas, but I do think it may be the quickest way to lure him out, and end this once and for all.'

Albert's gaze had again fallen to the ground as he listened to me, his face displaying less anger than before.

'Detective Matthews, it has been a very long night and I think we all need some rest. However if you would be so kind to meet us back here in the morning we can discuss this matter further with my wife. Good night.'

Albert turned abruptly and left the bar; leaving myself and Constable Taylor alone, neither one of us speaking as we got up and left the inn. Clearly Mr Summers realised that despite the danger involved with the task; he knew it was potentially the only way.

## Victoria

# CHAPTER 31

### THURSDAY 15TH FEBRUARY 1900

I barely slept at all that night. Every time I closed my eyes all I could see was *His* face. A cold pale face with deep menacing grey eyes, that caused you to feel naked and vulnerable beneath their stare. I could still feel his hands against my neck and shoulders, the sensation of which sent shivers down my entire body. How could a man, so normal looking, be capable of such horrific crimes to women? How could a man speak in such normal tone as though he was having but a simple conversation about the weather? Not once had he raised his voice, not once had he allowed anger to be felt in his words; yet the way in which he spoke frightened me, and I could not shake the image of him every time I closed my eyes.

Albert had not been alone with Detective Matthews very long last night, and returned to our room as I was finally getting into bed. He did not speak upon entering the room and kissed me swiftly goodnight before blowing out the single candle.

Now that morning had arrived I had planned to tell Albert how I wished to leave Whitby immediately, I would happily even miss breakfast if it meant we could leave sooner. There was a gentle knocking at the door; Albert who was already out of bed and sitting on the desk chair leapt to his feet straightaway to answer it.

'I am sorry to disturb you, Sir,' came the voice of Mr Walker, I could not see him from where I sat in bed but his distinct slow inert voice was instantly recognisable. 'I have just come to let you know that Detective Matthews has arrived in the bar and is awaiting you. He tells me you are expecting him.'

'Thank you Mr Walker, please let the Detective know we will be down shortly.' Albert spoke in such a matter-of-fact tone.

Albert closed the door and returned to the desk. He did not look at me directly as he began to speak.

'The Detective and I talked only briefly last night. I advised that he return this morning when you had had time to rest; that way any further discussions or questions could be had sensibly.'

I looked at Albert as he spoke, certain there was something he wasn't telling me.

'What more does he need to know? I was hoping we could leave today and go home.' I sat there in bed looking at him, hoping with all my heart that he would look at me and tell me what I wanted to hear. But he was silent, and simply stared out of the window, looking out onto Church Street. Eventually he broke the silence.

'Darling, the detective is under increased pressure to capture this man as quickly as possible. If there is anything we can do to help, then we must.' He finally looked at me, but it was not the look of compassion and hope that I was longing for.

Albert left me to get dressed, and I must admit that I did not rush myself to follow him down to see Detective Matthews.

As I entered the bar I saw that it was completely empty other than Albert, the Detective and Constable Taylor. They fell into silence as I walked into the room and looked at me awkwardly. I had been playing over in my head what the Detective could want from me again, and it was at that moment as all sets of eyes looked up at me in a particular way, that I finally realised exactly what it was.

'No!' My words broke the silence as I reached their table; all three men looked at me stunned.

'What is "No" for darling?' Albert asked in a rather cautious tone. 'You have not heard what the Detective has to say.'

'You want me to meet him; you want to lay out a trap to capture him don't you?' I demanded, and the expression on Albert and the Detective's face confirmed that I was indeed correct. I turned to leave, running back towards the stairwell, but Albert quickly bolted from his seat and took after me, finally taking hold of my hand as I placed my foot on the bottom step and stopping me from going any further.

'Please V, wait to hear what the Detective has to say. Just think of all the innocent women that could be targeted next if he's not stopped.' Albert paused, and I turned slowly to look at him. My entire body began to shake uncontrollably as my eyes filled with tears that did not fall; Albert pulled me in close and kissed my forehead as I tried to speak.

'I'm frightened.'


After what seemed like a very long time I eventually composed myself and agreed to listen to the Detective's plan, all the while quivering at the sheer thought of what could happen to me.

'Mrs Summers, I have been going over in my head the best possible way to do this. We need to ensure that D is completely unaware that anything is going to happen, and that you are purely there to meet him to leave. Now with him not giving you a time or place I was thinking that if you were to return to the bench below St Mary's Church, overlooking the East pier, then I believe he will not be far away.' The Detective spoke gently to me, like somebody relaying bad news; but my mind struggled to focus on his words.

'Now as you know Henrietta Street is a dead end, and your only way out will be to return to Church Street.' He did not wait for me to respond and continued relaying his ideas out to me. 'Myself and

Constable Taylor will both make sure to be close enough to ensure he does not give us the slip and that no harm comes to you. I will also arrange for back up officers to be on hand, just in case we need them.' I cradled a small china cup filled with tea that Mr Walker had brought over only minutes before, staring at it to avoid eye contact with Albert and the Detective. I suddenly realised that we were again sat in silence, the sound of Taylor's pencil still scratching away at his notebook. I looked up from my cup to find both Albert and the Detective looking at me; expectant expressions spread across both their faces waiting for me to respond.

'I understand your situation, Detective.' I placed the cup back into the saucer and looked him in the eye as I spoke. 'You are under enormous pressure to capture this man, and your own reputation lies in the balance if he is not caught. I did see the article in the Whitby Gazette referring to the incorrect arrest you made, that must have been very embarrassing for you I'm sure.' I paused to think where I was going with this; in all honesty my words were coming out much faster than I could think about them. Albert and Detective Matthews watched me as my words came out faster and faster, hope in their eyes that I was going to help.

'I have made my decision.' I suddenly declared; even I did not recognise the serious controlling voice that was coming from my lips. 'I will help in this matter, but please know this Detective; I am doing it for Whitby and the women who have lost their lives. Make sure it is clear that I am not doing this to help your reputation.' With that I stood, not fully sure why as I had no place to go.

'When do you suggest this all takes place Detective?' Albert asked before I could leave.

'To avoid as much disturbance and interference I think the streets of Whitby should be as quiet as possible, so that would mean sunset.'

Matthews looked at me, hopeful for a response.

'Sunset it is.' I said, quite matter of fact, before turning and returning to my room. I left the bar in quite a hurry, rushing back up into my room as I could feel the tears coming back to me. I slammed the door behind me, dropping to my knees before falling into panic-stricken sobbing. What have I done?

I did not leave the protection of the White Horse and Griffin for the remainder of the day. I felt cocooned within the walls of the inn, trapped like a prisoner, unable to leave and enjoy the delightful sea air that I had come to relish. Albert stayed with me inside our room the entire day, cancelling his final meeting so as not to leave me alone.

As the afternoon drew on, I began to become restless, my mind racing faster than it ever had before, petrified as to my fate. Albert ordered some hot water to our room so I could bathe, and lit a fire in the small wood burner situated in the corner of the room to keep me warm. As I lay silently in the warm water, Albert massaged my head; I could tell that he too was nervous about the upcoming events, although he was doing an extremely good job at portraying a relaxed state.

## Detective Matthews

# CHAPTER 32

I later returned to the station with Taylor where I had intended on relaying the new plan to the superintendent. We caught him on his way out to a meeting, and only had a couple of minutes to talk. He was pleased to hear I finally had something to work on.

'I don't care for details Matthews, just get back here with an update as soon as possible.' He barked at me.

'Yes Sir, however I do require a small number of officers to be on standby this evening.' He began ushering me out of the door.

'Yes, yes, do what you need to.' And with that he

slammed the door. Back in the foyer Taylor sat waiting for me, he has not said a great deal about the whole thing, and I was beginning to hope he was up for what lie ahead.

I had left Mr and Mrs Summers alone for the remainder of the day with a promise to return late afternoon, just before she would need to leave for the bench. I spent the remainder of the morning at the station with Taylor and four junior officers who I had managed to recruit for the evening. I knew tonight was not going to be as simple as just placing some handcuffs on a man and him come quietly. So a rest was something I desperately wanted, and was pleased to be able to go home for a short break in the early afternoon.

The morning frost on the ground had now gone, and the sky was bright blue with not a single cloud in the sky. By the time I reached home my fingers and toes were numb, and I immediately set going a coal and wood fire within my small living room; and it wasn't long before I was relaxing in my favourite chair in front of the fireplace, cradling a hot mug of freshly made tea. In no time at all I started dozing off, comfortable in the warmth of my sitting room and exhausted from the lack of sleep I had been experiencing.

I was abruptly woken by a large popping noise, but I soon realised it was a large wooden wedge cracking within the roaring fire. I found it difficult to fall back to sleep after that; the events of what were to come started racing through my mind, the images of events that were yet to come. Of all the cases I have ever been involved with, this was by far the worst. Never before in Whitby has a victim been set up as bait. Was I doing the right thing?

I spent the remainder of the afternoon at home, although I could not settle. My stomach felt twisted and uneasy, and my head began to throb with pain. I began pacing the house, constantly looking out of the windows as I passed them. My small terraced house only has two windows looking out to the front of the house, the living room which sees only the small road outside, and the bedroom window on the first floor which is just high enough to see over the houses opposite, and the view across towards St Mary's Church, and the magnificent Abbey. As I paced my worrying intensified. Was I setting Mrs Summers up for tragedy? Was I doing this for my own personal benefit so as not to be thrown off the case and deemed a failure throughout the town?

I went into my dark narrow kitchen and pulled out a bottle of whisky I hide under the sink for emergencies. Poured myself a rather large helping, and finished it in one mouthful. My self-doubt began to fade slightly and my nerves eased. I had a duty to the people of Whitby. If I let Mrs Summers leave town then who knows if another victim would be released as she had been. Who knows how many more women would have to die before this D was finally stopped? It was certainly a risk asking this of Mrs Summers, but I started to forgive myself into thinking it was the best possible way to bring this madness to an end.

There was suddenly a knocking at the door. I froze with shock. I hardly ever got visitors; who on earth could it be? I quickly placed my whisky back under the sink before heading through to the front door. I unlatched the door and slowly pulled it open, just wide enough to see who was there. Young Tom's smiling face peered up at me; but what was he doing here? Without a moment's hesitation I invited the boy in from the bitter cold, offering him a warm beverage as he entered into my sitting room. I had just recently replenished the fire as the February chill continued to turn my house into a frozen fortress.

'I'm sorry to disturb ya Detective,' Tom said after declining a drink. 'But I was told by Constable Taylor tha' ya were lookin' for me? He said I should see ya straight away.'

'Oh yes Tom, I was hoping to see you today.' I had completely forgotten I had needed to speak with him. 'Mr and Mrs Summers will be leaving Whitby this evening, after sunset, unfortunately this will be too late for a train, so we will require you to get the horses ready for them to leave.' Tom looked at me confused, but I was unsure how much more to tell him at this moment in time.

'No problem, Sir.' Tom responded. He wasn't stupid, and clearly knew the seriousness of the matter. 'Who be driving the coach, Sir?'

'I will be asking Mr Walker to drive them out of the town.'

'Please let me do it, Sir,' he spoke with such hope and eagerness to help, 'I promise I won't be of any bother.' I looked upon this young boy and smiled, I knew how much he had come to care for Mrs Summers and I could not bring myself to say no.

'Okay, Tom, but you must speak with Mr Summers and do everything he asks of you.'

'No problem Sir, I'll 'ave the horses ready for sunset an' awaitin' Mr and Mrs Summers.'

'Thank you Tom, Mr Summers will be with you first and give you the instructions.' Tom nodded and stood as though to leave.

'One more thing, Tom.' He turned back to me, his face turning serious upon seeing my own stern expression. 'I need you to keep this conversation to yourself; nobody is to know about the Summers' leaving Whitby this evening, do I make myself clear?' Again Tom nodded, and did not utter another word, before showing himself out.

I watched him from my window for a moment as he hurried along back down the street. I knew he could be trusted. He had taken a shining to Mrs Summers.

The blue sky of this morning had now turned overcast and grey as the North Sea winds had begun to pick up. It was shaping up to be a rough night.

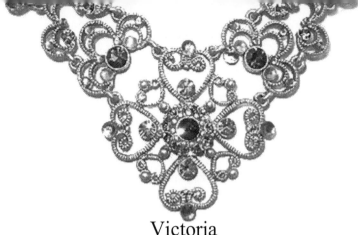

Victoria

# CHAPTER 33

By 5 o'clock I was getting ready to leave the inn. Detective Matthews and Constable Taylor had arrived around half past four to ensure we all knew the plan. He then left myself and Albert alone as he headed up Church Street to get into position. He did not want me to know exactly where he was planning to be, and he certainly did not want us to be seen walking up the road together.

Albert had been instructed to stay at the inn with Constable Taylor, where they could start loading our luggage onto the carriage and be prepared for us leaving promptly. Albert had argued this part of the plan quite strongly, but soon backed down once the Detective had explained how his being there may cause D to do something irrational.

'And where exactly are your police back up, Detective?' He questioned, before Matthews left.

'They are close by Mr Summers, and already in position ready.' The Detective said defensively, as he walked out of the door.

I wore my long black evening gown. The long sleeves and high neckline should be enough to keep me warm on this severely cold evening. I was also wearing the Whitby Jet necklace Albert had bought me; it somehow calmed me and made it feel as though Albert would be close by at all times. Black lace gloves covered my hands in hope to keep them warm, and a shawl around my shoulders for extra protection from the cold. My hair fell loose around my shoulders and I did not wear a hat as I typically would.

Albert slowly walked me to the inn door, his hand holding firmly onto my own. As we reached the threshold of the old inn Albert swung me into his arms and began kissing me passionately. My entire body was shaking as I held onto him for support. After a moment's embrace Albert finally released me, squeezing my hand gently again for reassurance and wordlessly nodding that everything was going to be all right. He was doing a good job at trying to stay relaxed for the sake of my feelings, but I knew my husband well, and I could tell he was just as nervous as I was. I lingered in the doorway a few seconds longer than necessary, hoping beyond anything that Detective Matthews would reappear and tell me the whole plan had all been cancelled.

As I exited the inn one last time I wished beyond anything it had been under better circumstances. I knew that once this ordeal was over Albert would be waiting for me with a carriage so we could finally go home.

Church Street was already quiet; and the last few people still wandering the street were making their way home before darkness fell once more. I was instantly hit by the cold wind cascading down the narrow cobbled street, the gust raced past my face causing my hair to blow dramatically behind me, and I had to hold firmly onto my dress to avoid it carrying me away. I began what now felt like a long walk along the street, battling against the wind that tried pushing me back, its force wrenching at my dress as though trying to stop me from going any further.

Upon reaching the end of Church Street I turned the corner and was met by the base of the 199 steps. Now deserted and lifeless the stone steps looked bleak in the fading light.

My pace was not as fast as it could have been as I continued along Henrietta Street. I could not help but look around cautiously at all the small houses that lined the narrow little street, wondering what they must have been like inside and who lived in them. I knew Detective Matthews had planned to be around here somewhere, hidden out of sight, and I presumed he would be in one of them; disguised behind a net curtain, camouflaged from sight, but hopefully in full view to come and help me as soon as possible. With every footstep I took my heartbeat began to quicken, my hands began to shake and my stomach uneasy. I took a deep breath and forced myself to keep walking, and as the road end came into view and the bench I was to sit and wait became visible, a nauseating sensation filled my entire body.

Sitting on the bench with the fury of the wind still hitting me, all I could do was look out onto the harbour entrance, still visible through the dimming light. The two stone piers, with their lighthouses mounted on the ends, looked strong and enduring as they took on the aggressive sea crashing against them. The sun had now completely set, and the final stream of light began to drain from the sky above. The sky was filled with what looked like one enormous dark grey cloud stretching from the horizon, right back over the little fishing town. I had been seated less than ten minutes when suddenly I heard footsteps from behind me. My heart skipped a beat as I continued to face forwards, staring hard at the West pier lighthouse which had at that moment began to cast its light out into the blackening open sea.

'I am pleased you finally made it my dear.' His voice was calm and collected as though greeting an old friend. I continued to face forward as he placed his hand casually upon my shoulder.

D.

# CHAPTER 34

I had been waiting all day for some kind of sign from her. I knew she would return to me, her body language was more than clear how much she longed for me. But as the day went on I began to fear the worst. Had that oaf husband of hers convinced her not to leave him, poisoning her mind with lies that she would be better off with him rather than me?

I knew it was unsafe to be seen during daylight now, so I spent most of my day in St Mary's churchyard. I had a perfect view of the harbour, and until I could think of the best way to rescue my sweet Victoria from the wicked man she called husband, all I could do was wait and hope.

The wind had increased quite dramatically as the day drew on. As dusk began setting in and the winds grew ever more I watched from the cliff top as fishermen secured their boats along the harbour. The River Esk very rarely saw this amount of current, yet this evening the river thrashed under the power of the sea winds.

Suddenly in the corner of my eye I saw somebody on the small street directly below me. I leaned over the cliff side to get a better view and was astonished to see that it was my Victoria; her hair was blowing beautifully in the wind as she sat perfectly still overlooking the river mouth before her.

Of course! Sunset is the perfect time to meet. Why had I not thought of this all along? She was clearly awaiting me so we could leave together in the romance of a sunset. Her idea is purely poetic and suitable for a love like ours, I must not leave her waiting in the cold, as we need to make our way as soon as possible.

I took off at speed in the direction of the 199 Steps, jumping down them a handful at a time, cautiously trying to judge the uneven surfaces just right in the dim light. As darkness began to engulf the streets of Whitby I knew that we would be relatively undisturbed leaving; and that by morning we would be long gone and living the life we both deserved.

As I approached, her delightful aroma filled my nostrils, my heart began to beat faster for her and I could not wait to touch her once again.

'I am pleased you finally made it my dear,' I said, touching her gently on the shoulder.

I walked around the bench to join her, all the while holding her shoulder in my hand. As I sat down she turned her head to face me, her eyes distant and sad as though trying to hold back tears.

'What is the matter? You should be happy that you can now be with me fully and not live the lie you once did. Albert will forgive you in time once he realises that this is where your heart truly belongs.'

She just stared at me for a moment before finally speaking, her voice croaky and with a slight tremor which I decided was due to the cold.

'I did not tell Albert I was leaving him' were her only words.

'Would you prefer he did not know? Do you just want to leave without saying goodbye?'

'No,' she said, her voice now harsh and cold, I looked at her with confusion in my face.

'Then what is it you plan to do?' I asked.

'I came to tell you that I have no intention of running away with you, I am in love with my husband, Albert, and I intend to leave with him, and him alone.'

My eyes widened at this statement. Clearly I am too late; she has had her mind twisted by that giant fool and has lost the spark and fight of what she truly wants in her heart. Me.

I took her by the hand, but she snatched it away just as fast. I had never seen her look at me in this way before, the anger and the pain she felt broke my heart. All I wanted for her was to be with somebody who loved her as much as she deserved, for her to live in happiness and with a man who knows exactly how she should be treated.

I am that man. I know I can make her happier than Albert and I had to prove to her that I wasn't going to give her up without a fight.

Detective Matthews

# CHAPTER 35

I sat and waited in one of the small cottages at the base of the 199 Steps, owned by the widow of a fellow police officer I once had the honour to work with. It had been many years since I had been in their front living room, and the conditions of my current visit could certainly have been better. I knew I needed to stay focused as I sat waiting for Mrs Summers to pass; D might arrive quite soon.

I kept going through every little detail in my head, questioning whether or not I was doing the right thing. I then started to wonder if D had seen me sneak into the little cottage; had he seen me leave the White Horse and Griffin only half an hour before Mrs Summers?

I watched from behind the curtain of the small window frame as Victoria passed me. I could not stop my hands from shaking as I watched her continue along Henrietta Street; her pace slow and hesitant. I knew this walk must have taken her a great deal of courage, and this alone filled me with the duty of making sure this man was finally caught, tonight.

All I could do now was wait, and hope that somebody else passed by; and thankfully I didn't have long to wait, as a gentleman in a long cape like coat came hurtling down the 199 Steps at such speed I thought at first he may have been falling. His large brimmed hat shadowed his face enough for me not to be able to identify him. He recomposed himself at the bottom of the steps, his back to me; and casually, as though no longer in a rush, he began walking the narrow cobblestoned road of Henrietta Street.

I decided to wait. I could not arrest a man simply for walking up the street. I needed to allow him to reach Victoria and start a conversation, and she needed to be the one to identify him. I was even contemplating waiting until both of them re-emerged from down the street. After all it was a dead end, where else could they go?

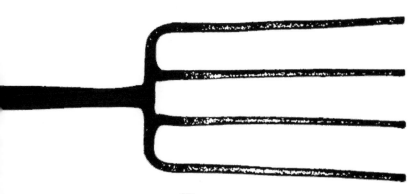

Tom

# CHAPTER 36

I was alone in the small stable yard besides the White Horse and Griffin when Mrs Summers left. I decided to stay out of sight until she had gone; emotions were high and I did not want to interfere as she kissed her husband and began heading along the road. That was my cue to bring around the two horses and carriage so that Mr Summers and Constable Taylor could begin loading the bags onto the back. Mr Summers had never been overly talkative to me on the best of days, but now as I helped him secure the luggage into place all he could do was look over his shoulder, back in the direction Mrs Summers had left.

The wind was awfully bitter this evening; even the horses were unsettled by it. Once the final bags were safety secured to the rear of the carriage I opened the door to offer Mr Summers a seat, away from the harassment of the wind.

'No thank you, Tom,' he said, his eyes fixated on the now empty road. 'I want to be seen by her when she returns.' I nodded and returned to the horses, whilst Constable Taylor spoke with him.

'It's a brave thing she be doing tonight.' Taylor said. 'You must love her dearly, Sir.'

'Yes Constable.' He smiled. 'I would be a lost man without her, for you see as much as I work, I work hard to ensure she has the best possible life. Not just her but her entire family I like to provide for as much as I can.'

'That must be an awful big obligation, Sir?'

'Yes, Constable, but I wouldn't have it any other way. You see when Victoria's father died only a few years ago I took it upon myself to see that her mother was well taken care of. You know, Victoria did not come from a wealthy family, and her father, who was a farmer his entire life, did not have anything of great value to leave behind after he had gone.'

'What did they do, Sir?' Taylor asked, his voice

cautious of not appearing too noisy.

'Victoria and I had been courting only a matter of weeks when her father died; she was working in a rather hostile pub in the centre of London. She lived in a small one bedroom house, which she shared with four other women, and sent most of her wage back to her mother.' His voice drifted slightly as though picturing it in his mind, his eyes firmly fixed on the road ahead looking out for his wife's return. 'Despite the fact that I am from a wealthy family and I could shower her with endless gifts, she refuses them all. She sees them as unnecessary, and sees that money can go to better use than a pair of ear rings she does not need. Sometimes it's almost like she feels unworthy of such nice things, but I also think it comes from growing up with little possessions that has made her feel she does not need them to be happy. Anyway, when her father passed I made a promise to her mother that I would send the money to them every week, and that Victoria was to save the money she made working at the bar for better living accommodation.'

I listened to Mr Summers talking about his wife to the Constable, and was in awe by how much he cared for her. The smile that flickered across his face when ever he said her name was sweet.

'Finally after a year of courting I proposed, and we were married only six months later, to the horror of my parents.'

'Why were your parents not happy Sir, did they not like... Mrs Summers?' It felt wrong of me to be listening in to their conversation; yet as he continued to speak about Mrs Summers to the Constable, the more interested I became.

'Oh they liked her, Constable, but they did not think her suitable for my wife. They had set up many of their wealthy friends' daughters with me, and none of them I liked very much. For you see they all reminded me far too much of my mother; highbrow, well-educated and quite frankly a huge braggart. Victoria however was different, she was fun and had a great sense of humour, and she certainly stood out against all of my other friends. Yet I loved her, and for some strange reason she loved me back.'

Listening to Mr Summers reminisce like this was strangely enjoyable to me, and I could tell that talking about it all made him think less about what was happening just around the corner. Constable Taylor seemed to realise this too as he continued to keep him talking.

By now the street was plunged into full darkness, and I lit the small lamp perched to the front of the carriage. Mr Summers eventually fell silent and continued to stare up the dark street, pacing occasionally to keep himself warm against the freezing cold wind that seemed to be getting stronger. The only sound coming from the heavy breathing of the two horses, and the whistling of the heavy wind as it rushed through small alleys.

All we could do now was sit and wait for Mrs Summers to re-appear.

Victoria

# CHAPTER 37

He took my hand but I snatched it away as fast as I could. He seemed shocked at my unwillingness at not going with him, hurt even, which was not at all what I had expected from him. I expected anger and rage, yet his face was saddened.

'I am sorry, D, but I think I should leave.'

I stood from the bench but he quickly reached out and grasped my hand again, pulling me back down onto the bench hard. He pulled me close to him and held the back of my head with his free hand, pulling me into him, he whispered into my ear, 'You would be making a big mistake returning to Albert, he will never love you as much as I do.'

He then inhaled deeply through his nose, his lips gently brushing against my neck as he did this. His lips found the delicate chain of my necklace and he stopped what he was doing immediately. He leaned himself back to get a better look at the jet pendant hanging from my neck. As he took in the sight of my necklace his expression did not change; his eyes lifted and found my own as he began to speak to me again.

'A gift from Albert?' He was not really asking this in the anticipation of a response, but simply confirming what he already knew.

'Yes.' I gulped as my body began to tremble with fear once more. He still held me close to him, his hands large and strong, I knew I could never escape his solid grip. I wished for Detective Matthews to get here and put a stop to this madness, now.

'If you are ever going to get over him my dear, you first need to remove him from your life; starting with this!'

D grabbed the jet pendant and pulled at it with an almighty force. My head lunged forward under the force, until finally the chain snapped off into his hand;

my neck stung instantly from the sheer force. D threw the necklace over the railing in front of us, and cackled a blood curdling laugh which rang loud into my ear, as we watched the necklace disappear over the edge.

'Now my darling,' he said, turning my face with force so we were looking directly into each other's eyes, 'your recovery begins, come let us disappear into the night where...' He stopped abruptly and looked over my shoulder.

'Does anybody know you are here?' he asked me, his tone harsh and accusing, all the while his eyes continued glaring passed me towards what little amount of Henrietta Street was visible from his position.

'No,' I lied, but he did not take in what I had said. His eyes were fixated on the small street behind me as though he was straining to hear something.

'We have company my love.' He spoke with a strange satisfaction in his voice. I listened out for footsteps, but heard nothing. How he could know somebody was coming up the street was beyond me: the bench sat nestled beside the final cottage, from here the narrow street was hardly visible at all, and I was certain that I couldn't hear any footsteps.

Suddenly he leapt to his feet, pulling me hard by

the hand and directing me away from the bench, the opposite way from Henrietta Street and down the steep slope towards the East pier.

'What are you doing?' I demanded, trying with all my energy to release my hand from his grip, yet his expression showed my efforts to escape were not causing any strain on him. As he steered me onto the large pier we became ever more exposed to the high wind coming of the sea. My large black dress acting like a ship's sail caught the wind and slowed me down, to the annoyance of D. My hair was blowing frantically in my face causing me difficulty to see and my heeled feet were occasionally tripping and stumbling as he dragged me along the uneven surface of the stone pier.

In a final bid to free myself I pulled hard on D's hand and to my surprise his grasp weakened and my hand was free from his. I did not have time to turn and run. D instantly retrieved my hand again. I retaliated and began to lash out at him, slapping him as hard as I possibly could against his chest and head. He tried to restrain me but I continued to hit him in the face. The high wind suddenly caught hold of my dress with an almighty force and I was thrown back from D, landing only feet away from the pier edge. There were no railings on this pier, just an almighty drop down to the fierce water crashing against the stone wall below. At the same time D's hat was also blown off by the wind, and took off over the side of the pier into the harbour below.

Anger filled his face, and D marched over to where I had landed and took me again by the hand. Dragging me to my feet he held me with both his hands firmly on my shoulders.

'Now hold on!' he shouted over the deafening wind, before again dragging me towards the end of the pier. What was he planning?

The pier was a dead end and the horrific weather was making it far too dangerous to be exposed between the rough sea and harsh harbour on either side of us.

'Stop!' I screamed at him. 'Have you no mercy?'

I began to struggle again from his grip, only this time he had hold of me tighter than ever. He turned back to look at me, his unruly curly hair now blowing into his face without the protection of his hat, and as he looked into my visibly scared face, he did something I was not expecting. He laughed. Not a small chuckle, or even a nasally amused laugh. No. He held up my hand to his face and laughed a cruel outburst of a laugh that carried itself in the wind, echoing back towards the cliffs behind me.

Suddenly his face turned rigid as his eyes focused on something behind me. A rage swept over him that until now I had never seen. His eyes seemed to turn darker and his lips pursed together so tight I thought at first he was in pain. I wanted to look at what he had seen but was too afraid to turn my focus from him. Without warning he reached out and grabbed me by the throat, twisting me around and pulled me in close to his own body; and it was at that point I could see Detective Matthews running down the steep slope and onto the pier; battling against the wind to maintain his balance.

'Let her go!' Matthews shouted, although it was almost inaudible through the vast wind blasting directly towards him, my eardrums sore as the harsh cold gale slapped against my face.

'Leave us be Detective, you cannot come between two people in love.' D's voice rang in my ear as he shouted back to Detective Matthews. His grip around my neck tightened and his other arm around me began crushing my chest under the strength of his broad torso and arm, his hold on me becoming tighter still. I let out a small scream that came out more like a gasp and I began to struggle and twist in a bid to free myself from within his grasp, but D just laughed at my pitiful efforts. Does this man have no compassion?

Matthews continued taking slow steps towards us, slow enough to hopefully not cause D any reason to do something thoughtless.

'Do not come any further...or I will...' D paused. He clearly did not have a plan, and I could feel that he too was trembling as he held me close.

'Just let Mrs Summers go and we can talk about this somewhere safe,' Matthews shouted over the blustery wind. At that moment he too lost his hat to the fierce harbour water.

'Leave us in peace!' D shouted, his voice trembling slightly, but Matthews took another couple of wary steps closer. Suddenly D released his grip of my neck; he began dragging me towards the edge of the pier. Holding onto the back of my dress he proceeded to hold me dangling dangerously off the edge; the waves crashed below, beating the pier hard with an almighty force. I screamed with fear and closed my eyes tightly shut so as not to see the horrendous fall that seemed apparent. I heard a muffled shouting come from

Matthews. D again burst into a roar of laughter as he threw me back onto the pier. I landed hard against the cold surface, slightly disorientated.

I saw Detective Matthews now standing only a handful of yards away, D shouting something at him, which I could not make out in the wind. Suddenly D turned and looked straight at me, dashing to my side and kneeling besides me.

'Are you all right my love? I am sorry if you were hurt. Once we rid ourselves of this man we can be together and alone.' Detective Matthews suddenly appeared behind D, grabbing him by the shoulders and pulling him backwards away from me. As he did this D's coat flung open and out fell a book, landing besides my leg. At first I did not take notice of this book: I was too busy watching as the two men began to scuffle along the ground, fists flying in all directions and both trying to be heard over the howling wind, although I could not make out what either of them were saying.

It was then I looked down at the book, I don't know why at that moment it suddenly intrigued me; it was bright yellow and hardbound. I picked it up and turned it over to look at the front. Staring up at me in blood red letters it read: Dracula by Bram Stoker. Why did D carry this with him? I had never heard of it and wondered why he would carry a book like this on him.

I saw peeking out between the pages what looked like a piece of paper, curious I pulled out the paper gently from the book and gasped upon recognising the pencil portrait of myself. Once hanging on the wall in D's hide, he now seemed to carry it with him.

I looked up from the drawing to see that D had pinned the Detective onto the ground, his hands around his neck suffocating the life from him. I needed to do something, I needed to help the Detective somehow; but what was I going to do to stop D who was so much stronger than me? I quickly jumped to my feet and raced over to them both. Lifting the heavy book above my head I smashed it around the side of D's head, causing him to fall sideways off Detective Matthews.

I hurriedly helped the Detective to his feet and looked back towards D who was crouched on the ground, his hand covering his left ear which had taken the brunt of my attack.

'Run Mrs Summers, I will hold him off, your husband is waiting with a carriage to take you away, now go, quickly!' Matthews screamed at me, but I was frozen to the spot with shock. Why wasn't I moving?

All of a sudden D got to his feet, blood trickling from his left ear, and his gaze immediately fell upon the book still in my hand; his eyes widened drastically upon realising what I held.

'Give it to me!' he shouted both arms outstretched.

Matthews stepped between us both to shield me. I was now the closest to the pier entrance, yet I did not run. I could see the fear in D's face, the panic of me now in possession of his book. A rage came over me, and I wanted to hit him with the book again. However seeing his face full of nerves, and his hands held out desperately wanting me to give it back to him, I did something that even I did not think I would have ever done.

'This is for all the woman you have hurt!' I screamed back along the pier at him, although exactly how much he heard over the wind I was unsure. I lifted the book above my head and threw it as hard as I could over the edge of the pier.

'Nooooo!' D cried, as he launched himself towards the edge of the pier, watching as his beloved book landed amongst the rolling waves below. Its yellow cover standing out against the grey murky water as it floated away.

I looked upon this man as he lay on the pier edge, and found myself pitying him. Clearly he had nothing in his life worth very much, and I had just tossed away the one possession that clearly meant something to him. This man clearly did not know his own mind. His actions he did not see as unreasonable and his desire for me came from the fact I was kind to him. He was clearly just very lonely, and very unwell.

At that moment his head turned and his eyes burned into my own as the anger seethed from every pore in his body, slowly he rose to his feet and began charging in my direction.

'You will pay for this,' he spat, 'you have caused me nothing but trouble.'

'Run. Now!' Matthews shouted before launching himself back at D to slow him down. I did not hesitate this time and quickly turned on my heels. The end of the pier was in my sight and I dared not look back once.

With the wind now behind me I was able to make it to the end of the pier and back up the steep incline towards the bench. I briefly stopped at the top to catch my breath where I momentarily looked back. Matthews and D were throwing punches at each other. I knew I needed to get back onto Church Street and out of D's sight as quickly as possible.

D.

# CHAPTER 38

I watched as my cherished book landed into the dark murky water below, my only treasured possession gone faster than I could have ever imagined. Signed by the author and held in his own bare hands, and now it was gone.

'You will pay for this,' I shouted at her. How could she betray me like this after everything we have been through? She had the opportunity to be free of the husband she clearly did not love, and be with me, her one true love.

I jumped to my feet in rage. This had to end now. I was beginning to tire of this craziness she was causing and despite my love for her I now realised that I would never be able to restrain a women of her mind and manner. If I cannot have her, then nobody can.

I made a dash to grab her, but the Detective jumped in the way. He started screaming for her to run, and to my astonishment she did. I grabbed Matthews by the throat and squeezed hard, his face turned red as his arms began to flail and swing at me; he then kicked me hard in the shin which caused me to release him as I crouched in pain for a split second. Suddenly Matthews charged at me again, punching me in the face and knocking me to the ground. He stood over me and before he could say anything I stopped him.

'Enough!' I shouted at him, and rose slowly to my feet once more. He paused and looked at me, and for a split second we both stood in silence. I could see in the corner of my eye Victoria had made it back up near the bench she had once sat, and continued out of sight as she headed back into town. I knew that time was running out.

'Leave the girl alone!' Matthews called to me over the now howling wind. 'You need to stop this madness. I know who you are.'

'You have no idea who I am.' I raced towards him

and grabbed Matthews by the collar of his coat, and in one final burst of energy I threw him as hard as I possibly could towards the edge of the pier. He landed with a heavy thud on the pier edge and looked up at me in pain as I towered over him. 'Do not pretend to know me, Detective. You think you know what is best for the people of this town, but you are wrong.'

Matthews tried to get up but I was too fast for him, grabbing him by his collar I lifted him up with both my fists, dangling him between the pier edge and the vertical drop below.

'Don't do anything stupid,' Matthews called out to me, his face filled with fear as he struggled against my grip. I did not say another word; I knew I needed to catch Victoria before I lost her forever. I let go of the Detective and watched as his toes landed on the pier edge, instantly losing his balance and falling backwards towards the crashing waves below.

I did not have time to even watch him hit the water; instead I started running as fast as I could back along the pier, and towards Church Street. I was sure that Victoria couldn't have gotten too far.

## Victoria

# CHAPTER 39

A s I raced along Church Street I was thrilled to see Albert standing outside the White Horse and Griffin with Constable Taylor. The two black horses were all ready to go, Tom was already sat in position, and the carriage was already loaded with our luggage. I ran straight into Albert's arm as he pulled me into his chest, holding me tight as he kissed me hard on the lips. Being in his arms again finally made my trembling subside, and my increased heartbeat started to ease.

Taylor opened the carriage door ready for Albert and me to enter.

'Where are the police back up officers?' I asked him as he ushered me into the carriage, 'Detective Matthews needs them.'

The Constable shrugged and his face turned to worry.

'I will leave you to go now, Madam, and I will head along to see that the Detective has the assistance he requires.' With that he closed the carriage door; I could hear his footsteps as he began marching back along the road.

I looked at Albert with concern spread across my face. I could not stop thinking about poor Detective Matthews facing that man alone.

'Do you think we should go back to help Matthews?' I questioned. 'We can't just leave him to face that monster alone, can we?'

'V, you heard what the Detective told us, you are to come back to the carriage and we are to leave immediately. I trust the Detective will have everything under control and Constable Taylor will make sure everything is all right.'

Albert spoke so convincingly I did not question him further, and leaned in closer to him to keep warm, placing the small blanket across our knees ready for the long journey ahead. At that moment the carriage began to move, and I watched as the front door of the White Horse and Griffin left my window view for the last time. I unexpectedly felt rather sad about our departure, despite all that had happened I had in fact liked Whitby and the little inn.

The carriage began to gain speed, going much faster than we would normally go. Albert leaned his head out of the small window, his intention to call up to Tom to slow down; however he was beaten to it as Tom shouted back first, his voice only just capable of being heard over the sound of the carriage wheels against the cobbled road.

'Hold on Sir, ma'am, and whatever you do don't look behind us.' Naturally Albert looked back immediately, and in a split second pulled his head back into the carriage and pushed up the window cover. He then quickly leaned over and slid my own window cover firmly into place.

'What is it?' I asked with a quiver in my voice; yet despite asking, in my heart I knew.

'He is chasing us' was Albert's response to my question. 'Now hold onto me tight.'

The carriage continued to gain speed, and the

rickety wheels began to shake violently against the un-evened road as the horses continued to gain speed. By now the entire carriage was shaking. I feared we would tip over at any second as I held onto Albert for dear life. Suddenly a loud bang hit the back of the carriage, and for a split second I feared one of the wheels had fallen off.

As the carriage continued to hurtle along the road, I soon realised the loud thud had come from the luggage rack attached to the back of the cab. D was on the rear of the carriage.

D.

# CHAPTER 40

I ran with all my speed and effort after her. She had clearly had a stronger lead than I had anticipated. As I hurtled past the 199 Steps and approached Church Street I could see the carriage pulling away from outside the inn. I raced as fast as I could in pursuit of them, desperate not to let her get away. I knew I needed to stop Victoria from making the biggest mistake of her life, returning to London with that man.

Constable Taylor was running towards me, his reaction shocked by the sheer sight of me. I ran directly at him and smashed into his chest, causing him to stagger backwards. Taylor lunged himself back at me, my patience diminishing as I saw the carriage near the end of Church Street. As Constable Taylor leapt forward to grab me again I hastily grabbed him by both shoulders and threw him against the side of the nearest building; his head smashing against a shop window. As he fell to the ground I stepped over him and continued my pursuit of the carriage.

Tom was on top of the carriage steering the horses and saw me racing down the street after them; he instantly began hollering at the horses to go faster. It wasn't long before the carriage was visibly shaking under the pressure of the speed against the cobblestones, yet the gigantic horses continued to race faster and faster along the road. I thought for a moment that I was going to lose them, but my own speed succeeded enough to keep me gaining on them.

My fingers outstretched as far as they could, I could almost reach the luggage rack perched on the back, and with an almighty push I launched myself upon them. My hand took hold of the smallest case strapped onto the top, and I was able to pull my feet in behind me.

The carriage continued to speed up and shake as I

tried to steady myself on the small rack, but I struggled to find a placing for my feet and balanced myself on the rack's corner, clinging onto the luggage securely tied against the cart.

'Victoria!' I shouted through the thin fabric that made up the carriage wall, but no reply was forthcoming. I need to stop the horses and get my Victoria away from the harm of this swaying rickety cart and away to safety; this dangerous driver was clearly trying to kill them all.

I tried to pull myself up higher in hope to see Tom sitting at the front, but as I maneuvered myself the wheels hit a large hole in the road, causing the entire carriage to buckle and shake. I heard Victoria let out a small shriek in terror. To hear her in distress caused my heart to ache, and I knew how much I desperately needed to stop the horses.

Still barely holding on, and with my feet still balanced onto the smallest remaining ledge, I decided to launch my entire body in a bid to push myself onto the roof, but as I did this my foot slipped against the shaking metal luggage rack and in the panic of falling, my hand grabbed out for anything to help stop me from plummeting to the ground. What I grabbed was the small case perched on top.

My legs were now dangling entirely off the back of the moving cart, and my grip of the bag was becoming weaker. I was determined not to give in, and with a final effort I tried to pull myself back up onto the rack; the small case which I clutched moved, and came apart from the remaining luggage. I fell backwards onto the road, the carriage speeding away as I landed hard on my back. I lay there for a moment, winded and sore, my ankle stinging from landing on it at an awkward angle. As I looked up I saw the carriage race around the corner out of sight. I had lost her.

Victoria

# CHAPTER 41

FRIDAY 16TH FEBRUARY 1900

It was late afternoon when we finally arrived home in London. It was raining heavily and I was pleased and relieved when I finally stepped through my own front door. As expected Albert and I were exhausted, the night time traveling had taken a long time, and it was it not until mid-morning that we finally managed to get a train home from York.

For the past few hours Albert and I had barely spoken, and the carriage ride from the station to our house had seen us both almost asleep; the darkened circles forming around our eyes a brutal hint at just how exhausted we were.

We lived in an end townhouse which overlooks a rather large green that is frequently used as a cricket pavilion. Upon entering I took myself straight upstairs to our bedroom; I had not had chance to change my clothing since being on the pier and desperately wanted to clean myself up. My own bedroom was a welcome relief to me, and as I opened the large double wardrobe I decided that what I really wanted was to get into my nightgown. A gentle knock on the bedroom door shocked me from my trance. I opened the door to be met by another tired little face.

'Sorry to disturb ya Miss, but where would ya like these cases?'

'Just in the corner here will be perfect.' I pointed besides the window. 'Thank you for bringing them up for me, Tom.' His smile was still warm and gentle despite his clear exhaustion.

'Would ya like anything else Ma'am?'

'Please call me Victoria, Tom, and no I do not wish you to do anything other than freshen up and have a rest. You are not here to serve me remember; this is your home now.' His smile widened and his eyes lit up as he leaned in and threw his arms around my waist, holding into the tightest hug his tired little body could manage.

'Thank you Miss…Victoria.'

Tom had driven the carriage all the way to York that night, and even helped carry the luggage along to the platform where we waited for such a long time. Despite me telling Tom to go back to Whitby, he would not, "not until I 'ave seen ya safely onto the train" he had said. It was bitterly cold in the station, and the blanket was soon laid out across all three of our laps. Tom fell asleep soon after and as I watched him sleep my heart ached at the thought of him returning to Whitby. Homeless and barely protected in his shabby clothes. I had asked Albert if we could offer him a home, and at first he was reluctant; however the train was not for many hours, and I soon managed to persuade him.

Tom left my bedroom and I was alone again. I picked out one of my soft silk nightgowns from the wardrobe and laid it out onto the bed. My eyes scanned my bedroom; the large framed window was being bombarded by the heavy downpour that had begun, and the dark overcast clouds were causing the room to grown dark in the dim light. I stood in complete silence, stroking the silky soft texture of my nightgown, enjoying the silence of my own room. No seagulls crying, no waves crashing against the pier, and no Him.

I unbuttoned my heavy dress and allowed it to simply fall to the ground, and as it fell, my eye caught sight of a piece of paper that also landed onto the ground with it. I gasped loudly in shock even before picking it up. I unfolded the paper to inspect it further, and before me was the perfectly drawn portrait of myself. As I stared at the picture for what felt like a long time, my eyes slowly filling with tears as the reality of what happened on the pier suddenly came back to me; and without warning I burst into uncontrollable sobbing.

There was another gentle knocking at the door.

'Are you alright darling?' It was Albert. I quickly folded the piece of paper and stuffed it into my wardrobe, as far back as physically possible. I then snatched myself a tissue from the box next to my bed and dried my eyes to the best of my ability.

'Come in,' I called out, and Albert entered the room, instantly recognising that I had been crying. He strode over to where I stood and scooped me up into a passionate embrace, softly moving the stray hairs that now covered my face and looked me in my tear filled eyes.

'It's over now V, you're safe.'

D.

# CHAPTER 42

I never returned to Whitby again after that night.

After falling off the moving carriage it had taken me some time to get back to my feet. Victoria was now long gone and so I began to walk. No real destination in mind. I just knew that Whitby no longer served a purpose to me, and that staying was the wrong thing to do.

The small suitcase which I had pulled off the carriage I carried with me as I strode the entire night. When I finally stopped walking it was daylight, and the sun illuminated the Yorkshire moorlands that surrounded Whitby. The North Sea was no longer visible, and the majestic Abbey ruins that normally dominated the landscape had disappeared from the horizon. At this moment in time I had no idea where I was or where I was going. I stopped to rest, my legs becoming tired and my ankle swollen slightly from my fall. I needed somewhere safe I could rest.

With daylight now on my side, I decided to inspect the case, and was pleasantly surprised with what I found. Attached to the handle, was a small leather tag, and within the tag read:

Mr & Mrs Summers

13 Vincent Square

London

And at that point, I knew exactly where my destination was going to be.


To Be Continued…

Continue the story now with
D: Revenge Hits London
**OUT NOW!**

ALSO...

THE PLANTING OF THE PENNY HEDGE

A DETECTIVE MATTHEWS NOVEL

IS OUT NOW!

# About The Author

Chris Turnbull was born in Bradford, West Yorkshire, before moving to Leeds with his family. Growing up with a younger brother, Chris was always surrounded by pets, from dogs, cats, rabbits and birds…the list goes on.

In 2012 Chris entered into a Civil Partnership with his long term partner, since then Chris has relocated to the outskirts of York where he and his partner bought and renovated their first home together.

Chris now enjoys his full time employment at the University of York and spends his free time writing, walking his Jack Russell, Olly, and travelling as much as possible.

For more information about Chris and any future releases you can visit:

www.chris-turnbullauthor.com
facebook.com/christurnbullauthor
Twitter: @ChrisTurnbull20
**Praise for**

# The Vintage Coat

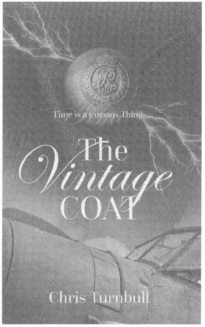

This book is a little gem, filled with surprises. It has a refreshing almost innocent quality about it. The Vintage Coat gives us romance, adventure, family ties, friendship and sacrifice. The concept of a time-travelling coat is unique and is a testament to the authors originality and imagination.

- DM Singh:   Author of Regina: The Monster Inside

A story of family & friendships, you cannot help but fall in love with the characters. I truly felt the fun & sense of adventure that Joseph (our main character) experiences slipping back in time. The author also made me sympathise with Joe and experience his heartache.

- Rose English: Author of One Breath

The easiest 5 stars ever given, this book got me hooked from the very first page. It was so well described that you actually feel like you were there in Alston yourself. I would recommend this book to anyone - you will not be disappointed, and the twist at the end is so unexpected it leaves you wanting more.

- LJ Wright

# Acknowledgements

I would firstly like to thank my long suffering husband, who must have read this book so many times during the editing process.

Secondly I would like to thank Haley and Stuart, who kindly allowed me to stay at their home in Whitby for two nights. Here I wrote the final six chapters of the book in the perfect location.

I would also like to thank Dawn and Pete from Follow This Publishing, without your continued support I would never have published The Vintage Coat, and your continued support of my writing means a lot to me.

Lastly I would like to thank everybody who read The Vintage Coat – your reviews on Amazon and Goodreads are very much appreciated, and seeing them all and the love you have shown towards me and my book was overwhelming. For that reason you encourage me to keep writing, and publishing.

Thank You!

## Behind The Darkness

Many people have asked me how I managed to write this book so quickly, commenting that Whitby's Darkest Secrets release was only 7 months after The Vintage Coat, however this is not the case. WDS was in fact started in the summer of 2013, and came from the simple idea of wanting to base a story in one of my all-time favourite places.

My first memories of visiting Whitby were on a group weekend with the boy scouts. During which I joined in with a Dracula fancy dress evening whilst attending one of the famous Whitby Ghost Walks.

From then on my love of Whitby grew, and I have visited the small fishing town numerous times over the years, from day trips to longer stays.

Developing the characters for WDS has been one of the highlights, and using them to tell the story allowed me to delve into their inner most feelings.

The first draft of this book was completed earlier in 2015, when I stayed in Whitby for two nights. I walked around the ruined abbey, which strangely I had never done before, and walked the streets to really get into the emotions, sights and smells the characters would face – minus the 1900 smog.

Book One of the Trilogy

# Regina: The Monster Inside
## DM Singh

What if what you were could destroy everything and everyone you loved?

Regina thought she was an average teenager. When strange things start to happen, she discovers she belongs to a hidden world of supernatural beings and she is the most dangerous of them all.

Her existence is a death sentence to her, her survival could be a death sentence for us all.

Will those who fear her destroy her and those she loves, or is she destined to become the monster within?

Join the fight for survival.

http://authordmsingh.weebly.com/

Printed in Great Britain
by Amazon